By SARAH ELLIS

The Several Lives of Orphan Jack
The Young Writer's Companion
Back of Beyond
Out of the Blue
The Baby Project
Pick-Up Sticks
Next-Door Neighbours

ODD MAN OUT

ODD MAN OUT

Sarah Ellis

GROUNDWOOD BOOKS
HOUSE OF ANANSI PRESS
TORONTO   BERKELEY

Groundwood Books / House of Anansi Press
110 Spadina Avenue, Suite 801, Toronto, Ontario M5V 2K4
Distributed in the USA by Publishers Group West
1700 Fourth Street, Berkeley, CA 94710

We acknowledge for their financial support of our publishing
program the Canada Council for the Arts, the Government of
Canada through the Book Publishing Industry Development
Program (BPIDP) and the Ontario Arts Council.

Library and Archives Canada Cataloging in Publication
Ellis, Sarah
Odd man out / by Sarah Ellis.
ISBN-13: 978-0-88899-702-9 (bound)
ISBN-10: 0-88899-702-7 (bound)
ISBN-13: 978-0-88899-703-6 (pbk.)
ISBN-10: 0-88899-703-5 (pbk.)
I. Title.
PS8559.L57O33 2006   jC813'.54   C2006-901805-7

Cover illustration by Karine Daisay
Design by Michael Solomon
Printed and bound in Canada

For Donna, Deirdre, Ariel and Robin —
three generations of excellent women.

Thanks to Chris Kerluke, who asked for a
book about espionage, and to Lewis Lopes,
who thought of the title.

With thanks to the Canada Council for the
Arts, which last year invested $20.3 million
in writing and publishing throughout
Canada.

INTRODUCTION

"INSERT THE BUCKLE into the metal fitting and tighten the belt snugly about your hips." The flight attendant held the seatbelt up high for all to see.

Kip inserted and snugged and pulled his notebook out of the seat pocket in front of him.

RAQ (Rarely Asked Question): Who doesn't know how to use a seatbelt?

A: Once upon a time there was an extremely old hermit lady. She had lived her whole life on a tiny farm in northern Ontario with sheep and goats and chickens. She grew all her food and knitted all her clothes. Her name was the Lone Ethel. One day she got a letter from her long-lost brother. He lived in Victoria and he was dying and he wanted to see his sister one last time. He sent her a plane ticket and some money. The Lone Ethel packed her knitted clothes into her knitted suitcase and walked twenty kilometers to the highway. Then she got on a bus to Toronto. Then she got on a bus to the airport. The Lone Ethel had never traveled in a car.

Therefore, when she got on the plane she did not know how to use a seatbelt.

Done. One page. Kip snapped the notebook shut. Homework done and the plane was still taxiing down the runway. Four and a half hours at a cruising altitude of thirty-one thousand feet. Air above and air below and air all around. Four and a half hours away from his destination, from Gran and the island.

ONE

KIP'S EYES jumped open. Four o'clock in the morning and he was awake. Not just awake but super-awake, like some martial arts master — alert, energetic, ready to spring into action.

Gran had warned him. "Jet lag. You might wake up really early because your body will think it's three hours later. I'll leave you the remote and some snacks."

He stretched out his legs to the end of the couch and peered around the dimly lit living room full of the shapes of alien furniture. There wasn't much action to spring into.

Today he would meet the cousins. They had been asleep last night when he and Gran arrived about midnight. Five girl cousins. Mom said he had met them before. He didn't remember. Or maybe he remembered one of them tying him up with the belt from her bathrobe and pretending to burn him at the stake. But maybe he just remembered Mom telling that story.

He pulled his notebook out of his pack and swiveled around on the couch to let the moonlight shine on its pages.

RAQ: How do you know what is really remembering the truth and what is remembering a story?

A: True remembering is not as tidy as stories. Maybe.

Kip eased the lid off the plastic bowl of snacks and extracted a large perfect chip. Sour cream and onion. Was it really as good as it seemed? He thought of the scientific method. Hypothesis and testing. He clicked on the TV and cruised the world of early-morning television as he retested the chips to the bottom of the bowl.

Theory confirmed. Even the chip dust licked off a wet finger was excellent.

RAQ #2: Why do the women on the New Brunswick Ladies' Bowling Team all have names of one syllable, and (RAQ #2A) who is watching the National Women's Bowling Championships at 4:30 A.M. except me?

A: All the husbands and kids and parents and in-laws and cousins of Flo, Em, Shirl, Jo and Sue are watching, and they call them that because you don't waste syllables in New Brunswick.

Kip flopped back on the couch. He brushed chip crumbs off the pillow. Rain gusted against the window. The darkness was lifting.

Wednesday and no plans, no schedule, no school. Nothing he had to do.

Weird. In bed on an island. Water above and water all around.

Toward dawn there was a show about Mongolian yurts. Kip knew he had heard the word yurt, but if he had thought about it at all, which he couldn't remember doing, he would have said it had something to do with dairy products, like yogurt. In normal waking hours with a normal brain, he would have flipped right past an instructional documentary. But with jet-lag brain there was something soothing about watching three people building wooden supports to make the bones of a tent. There were many slow close-ups of hands slipping rafters onto a central ring. The builders were three silent men.

As the canvas was being strapped on, Kip's eyes fell shut.

* * *

Slipping and sliding down a bowling lane, Kip tried to snatch the end of a dream, but it whipped around the corner of the morning and was gone. There was a chirping and giggling outside the door, then Gran's voice. "Don't wake him."

Kip rubbed his eyes, licked the inside of his sour-cream mouth and pushed himself off the couch. He opened the door.

Sitting on the floor were two skinny girls wearing ballet outfits.

"We weren't waking you up," said ballerina the first.

"We were just singing like birds," said ballerina the second, "to welcome the day."

"Do you like it here?" said Ballerina I. "Is it better than Ontario? How come you never came here before?"

Another girl, bigger and more regular looking, stepped into the hall and spared Kip from replying.

"Aubade," she said. "A piece of music appropriate to the dawn. I'm Hilary. I once tried to burn you at the stake but I've outgrown that. That's Jane. That's Daffodil. Did you have any good dreams?"

Dreams? Did she really say Daffodil? Kip was rescued a second time by Gran announcing breakfast.

The kitchen contained Gran, watery sunshine and a table covered in cereal boxes. It also contained two more girls. One was eating out of a dog dish. One was sitting on top of a stepladder.

Were there more? No, five would be right. Five cousins.

Opera was blasting out of the radio, and the yellow walls seemed to be covered in writing. Kip felt like the Lone Ethel or a visiting alien.

Ballerina II slid onto a chair and picked up a box of cereal.

"What are the three periods of the Mesozoic Era?" she asked.

Everybody ignored her, and she didn't seem to care.

"Cretaceous, Jurassic and Triassic," she announced to nobody and started to pour her cereal.

"Listen up," said Gran. "This is Kip. Unless you want another name for the holidays. Do you, Kip?"

{14}

"Er, no, I don't think so."

"Okay. Here's who's who." Gran pointed. "Hilary, Alice, Emily — "

"I'm a dog," said the smallest girl, spooning cereal out of the dog dish, "but I speak human."

"Right," said Gran. "I keep forgetting. Emily is a dog. We don't know if this is permanent. Where was I? Emily, Jane and Daffodil (otherwise known as Betsy). The monstrous regiment of women."

Kip tried to match names and bodies. Alice — on the ladder. Emily — a dog. Hilary — tall. Jane — Ballerina I, blonde hair. Daffodil — Ballerina II, black hair.

"I'm Jane's twin," said Daffodil.

"No, you're not," said Alice. "You're not even sisters. Jane's my sister."

"She is too my twin. We're both nine."

"That's like saying Kip is my twin because we're both twelve," said Alice.

Twelve? thought Kip. How come she's so big?

"Oh, come on," said Daffodil. "He can't be your twin. He's a boy!"

"Plus he's adopted," said Emily.

"Just like me," said Daffodil.

Adopted! I'm not adopted. Kip felt like he had wandered into a madhouse.

"Kip's not adopted," said Gran. "What gave you that idea?"

"Oh, yeah, I forgot. He has a stepfather. I knew it was something like that."

The opera ended in a chorus of hysteria, and a narrow crack of silence appeared.

"All my grandchildren," said Gran. "For a whole month. This is heaven on a stick."

Emily jigged up and down on her chair. "Can we do the room lottery now?"

"Breakfast first," said Gran. "Help yourself to cereal, Kip."

"Then can I tell him the food rules?" said Alice.

Gran poured herself a cup of coffee. "Shoot."

Alice climbed down from the ladder, pulled it squeaking along the floor and then scurried up again. She took a black felt pen out of her pocket and pointed at the list of rules written on the wall, to the right of the door.

"Number one…" she began.

"He could just read them himself," said Hilary. "Can you read, Kip?"

What kind of a question was that?

"Of course," said Kip.

"They ask that because I can't read," said the dog. "I can't read even though I'm seven. I might never read. I'm more oral."

"Ahem, ahem," said Alice from on high. "Rule number one: Gran cooks once a day. Like it or lump it. Rule number two: Eat anything you want for breakfast and lunch. Gran does not do nutrition for grandchildren on holiday. Rule number three: Clean up after yourself. That means — 3A: Wash it. 3B: Dry it. 3C: Put it away. Everything. Every time. If you don't…"

"Keelhauling!" yelled a chorus of cousins.

"Questions?" said Gran.

Kip had about seventy dozen questions. He grabbed one at random.

"What's keelhauling?"

"It is totally gross," said Alice. "You drag a person through the water under the bottom of a boat. And the boat is covered with barnacles so it's like a total body grater. Mean captains did it to sailors. Of course, Gran doesn't really have a boat."

"But I could rent one in a second," said Gran. "One dirty teaspoon in the sink and I'm off to the marina."

"*Now* is it time for the lottery?" said Emily.

"Okay," said Gran. "But we had better give Kip a tour of the house first so that he knows what the stakes are. Get dressed and muster at the front door."

Kip retreated to the living room and closed the door to an indignant ballerina duet of "But we *are* dressed!" His head was buzzing.

A phrase popped into his mind. The female of the species. He was used to females. Correction: he was used to one female, his mother. Just the two of them. Except it wasn't just the two of them anymore.

Kip put that thought in a box and shelved it.

TWO

THE TROOPS were mustered. The ballerinas had added warm-up leggings to their outfits. Emily had a leather collar around her neck. Alice was carrying a folding step stool and a fat felt marker.

"What about the coal hole?" said Hilary.

"This is a huge house," said Gran. "Nobody needs to sleep down in the coal hole."

"Dogs like the coal hole," said Emily.

"Nobody is sleeping in the coal hole," said Gran.

Alice climbed up on the step stool and stretched to write above the door, *No dogs in coal hole.*

"Right," said Gran. "First choice, the cubby."

A small room off the front hall was filled with a cot, a dresser and a rod for hanging clothes.

"Features," said Hilary. "Privacy and plenty of hangers. The cubby is sweet."

"Is sweet good?" said Gran.

"Wooka good," said Hilary.

"And the front door is close for when you need to go out for walkies," said Emily.

Kip found himself beside Hilary as they all marched up the first flight of stairs. The walls of the staircase were covered in bits of written-out music.

"What's that?" asked Kip.

"That's mine," said Hilary. "Blues songs for the house."

"How come you're allowed to write on the walls?"

"Because the house is going to be torn down after this summer. Didn't you know? That's why we're all here. Last chance to be together in the old house."

That's not why I'm here, thought Kip. Shelve it.

"I knew she was moving but I didn't know about the house."

Hilary nodded. "Gran says nobody wants a big old house like this. So we get to do whatever we want. The little ones think it is totally great. But I'm not so sure. I've been here every summer. I'm going to miss it. That's why I'm writing blues on the walls."

Alice tore by them to the top of the stairs and then slid down the bannister.

"Gran, can I saw off the knob at the bottom so I can go right off the end?"

"We'll discuss it," said Gran.

The first floor landing was decorated with a large hand-drawn map of the world. Kip looked more closely. Not exactly the world, *a* world. There were continents, islands, oceans, rivers, lakes, cities, little pointy caps of mountain ranges. Some of the places had familiar names. Narnia, Avalon, Atlantis, Mordor. Some were strange — Ishmaelia, Jabberwocky Wood, the Slough of Despond.

"That's Gran's," said Alice. "She calls it Make Believeia. You can ask about any of the places."

"What's the Rootabaga Country?" said Kip.

Emily groaned. "Don't ask, don't ask. We need to choose the rooms."

"I'll tell you about it later," said Gran.

Room two, second floor, had racing-car wallpaper and double doors that led out to a wet tarpaper-covered deck. Room three had cupboards on every wall.

"The best thing about this room," said Alice, "is that you can bivouac on top of the cupboards."

"You mean sleep there?" said Gran.

"Yup," said Alice. "Stick a piton in the wall and rope yourself in."

"I won't ask how you know this," said Gran.

Room four was the biggest, with flower bouquet wallpaper and a closet with a window.

"Hey, Gran," said Emily. "Know how dogs claim their territory?"

"Yes," said Gran, "and if you're thinking what I think you're thinking then don't even think it."

Alice pulled out her marker and wrote on the door frame, *No peeing in corners*. The chorus of "Yuck! Bleck! Gross!" had barely died away before they entered option number five, the screened-in porch.

"Small but airy," said Hilary.

"Okay, troops," said Gran. "Onwards and upwards. Excelsior!"

"Upwards?" said Jane indignantly. "We've never used the attic before."

"That's because it used to be cram jam full of junk," said Gran. "But I have cleared the decks. Morris the junk man came over and I gave him the lot. Wait until you see. It is a veritable poem of emptiness."

Kip trudged behind the group to a set of narrow stairs. What did Excelsior mean? Should he ask? Nobody else seemed to pay a bit of attention.

Kip shook his head to clear it of words. At home he and his mother thought things out before they said them. Gran and the cousins just seemed to let the words inside their heads spill right out of their mouths. Was this a girl thing?

The attic was closed off with a trap door over the stairs. Gran pushed it open ahead of her and secured it with a hook. The girls exploded upwards.

The ballerinas started to slide across the linoleum, squealing.

Hilary started to sing, "Nobody knows the trouble I've seen…"

"This was your dad's territory," said Gran to Kip in a low voice. She lowered the trap door with a rope and pulley. Painted on the back of the door, in beautiful even white letters, were the words, *No dragons allowed on the drawbridge.*

"He did that," said Gran. "Always good with lettering."

A heavy, fast, invisible soccer ball smacked Kip in the chest.

He knew those letters. He knew that *e* with its extra flip. He knew that slanting *o*. *Master Kip Coulter Esq.* Fancy letters painted in gold on the toy box that sat beside his bed at home. He knew those letters in his fingertips. He used to get out of bed at night, in that time after Dad died, and sit in front of the box, running his fingers over the letters glowing faintly in the night-light. He sat on the bedside rug pretending that he was painting, pretending that his hand was Dad's hand, pretending that Dad was coming home soon and that there was no such thing as black ice.

Dad-words. Kip wanted to do it again, to trace the letters on the trap door with his fingers, to feel some little leftover molecule of his father in the white paint or in the watery sunbeams. But a ballerina came by in a grand jêté. A dog was down on all fours sniffing the corners. A climber was gunk-holing up a door frame and Gran was trying to herd everyone back downstairs.

Kip knew what he needed. This place. He needed to be up here alone.

Back in the kitchen, Gran eyed the dirty cereal bowls.

"Those barnacle wounds really sting in the salty seawater."

"Can't I just lick out my dish?" said Emily.

"No," said Gran. "Dogs need a clean dish for every meal. For optimum canine health."

Alice groaned. "But we can't wait another *minute* for

{22}

the room lottery. We will *die*. Can't we do it later?" She looked around for support. There was a chorus of nods, cries of pain and one dog howl.

"Okay, okay. Grab a seat, everyone."

Gran produced six slips of cardboard and started writing on them. "As usual, it is a random draw. Questions?"

Kip jumped in. "Why don't we just choose rooms?"

"Ha!" said Gran. "We used to try that and it led to rancor, armed stand-offs, rivalry…"

"And big fights," said Daffodil. "I didn't like that."

"It was janky," said Hilary.

"Is janky bad?" asked Gran.

"Wooka bad."

"Anyway, once we had to have an outside mediator," said Gran. She fanned out the pieces of cardboard like cards in a card trick. "Kip gets to choose first."

"Why?" demanded Alice and Emily in a single voice.

"Because he is an oppressed minority."

Gran held out the fan of cards to Kip.

"Bonne chance," she said, and she gave him a very subtle wink.

Then he noticed that one of the cards was nudging out a bit. He grabbed it.

"Attic," he read out.

Cries of delight and disappointment rang out, but he didn't pay any attention. He washed his bowl to save his skin and went off to claim his territory.

THREE

K IP CARRIED his dufflebag and his pack up to the attic. He lowered the drawbridge with the pulley.

The air was still and warm. A folding cot, still folded, sat in the corner of the landing with the sausage of a sleeping bag perched on top. There was no other furniture. No furniture, no curtains, no pictures, no cousins, no talk. Just three rooms of air and questions.

Kip looked toward the door to the front room and noticed a key in the lock. Better and better.

He pushed the cot down the hall, squeaking over the worn linoleum to the center of the room. He opened it out and lay down with his head on the rolled sleeping bag, staring upwards. He took a deep breath and invited his father to join him in the silence.

Tristan James Coulter. *Tragic Traffic Fatality.* That was what it had said in the newspaper. A patch of black ice. A tree. Nobody's fault. No rhyme or reason. He died on the day that Kip took the Friday snack to kindergarten.

Kip remembered the snack — red jelly stars — but he did not remember hearing the news.

Dad was made out of pieces. Jelly stars, photo albums, Mom's stories and Kip's own scattered memories — memories of big hands, of standing on the front of Dad's skis, of having the bubble-bath pretend-shaved from his cheeks.

And now, another piece. This place. Tristan Coulter slept here. He saw the sky through the leaves of that tree through that window. He stared at that ceiling.

No dragons allowed on the drawbridge. Did he pretend he was in a castle tower? Did he pretend he was a knight?

A pale green glass shade hung from the ceiling. There seemed to be a kind of decoration around the plate where it was attached, like a circle of lace. Odd. Everything else in the room was totally plain.

Kip stood up on the cot and tried to get a better look. Too far and too small. He needed something taller to stand on.

There was Alice's step stool, but he didn't want to face the girlatorium downstairs. He scissored the cot back into its folded position and climbed up on it. It was wobbly, and he had to rest his hand on the ceiling to steady himself.

Not lace, but numbers. Small and neat, written in ink around the edge of the light plate, on the white plaster ceiling.

4753596167717379…

Kip shifted to see the rest of the sequence. The cot

tipped and skittered off under him, and he crashed loudly to the floor.

Whoever called it the funny bone had a sick sense of humor. Kip held his elbow and jumped around for a while. Then he sat on the overturned cot.

Was it one of the wall-writing cousins? *No dogs in coal hole.* No, it was too neat and too…serious.

Kip thought of Gran's low voice. "Your dad, always good with lettering." It must have been him.

Kip shivered. But why? Why numbers that didn't mean anything? Maybe they made sense if you could see them all.

Worth braving the female of the species.

* * *

Hilary was in the kitchen whipping cream with a whisk and singing along to her Discman. When she noticed Kip, she pulled her headphones off her ears.

"Gran's gone to the store with Emily and Alice. We'll go to the beach later if it stops raining."

There was a crash and a war cry from the dining room. Kip jumped.

"What's that?"

"Oh, Jane and Daffodil are bashing out part of the wall with a sledgehammer."

"They're allowed to do that?"

"Yup. We're just not allowed to saw through beams, in case the house falls down. The rules are around here somewhere." Hilary gestured largely to the graffiti'ed walls.

Kip spied the step stool propped beside the fridge.

"Can I borrow this?"

"Sure. So, do you like the attic?"

Kip nodded. "It's…sweet."

Hilary stopped her whipping.

"I was wondering, if it's not too snoopy or anything …what's Uncle Orm like?"

Uncle Orm. Orm. Kip stood in silence. From Hilary's headphones came the sound of mice singing inside a tin can. What Orm was like was parsnip casserole surprise, a plantar wart or an oral book report. Put up with it. Hope it eventually goes away. Don't think about it. Shelve it if you can.

"He's okay."

"I just wondered because, like, he's the first stepfather in the family. Well, the first step-anything, really. So we were just wondering what it was like."

"It's okay."

"Gran says we get to meet him when he and your mom come to get you, after the honeymoon in Hawaii."

Honeymoon? Kip's brain stalled. Mom hadn't said it was a honeymoon. But of course that's what it was. She just hadn't used that word. It's what people did after they got married. What a stupid word. Might as well say jam-sun, or peanut butter asteroid or Cheez Whiz —

There was a noise at the door.

Hilary tapped the whisk against the edge of the bowl and handed it to Kip.

"Quick, they're home. Take this and disappear before we have to figure out how to divide it six ways."

Kip took the stool and whisk up the back stairs.

His tongue finished its thorough mining of whipped cream, and he positioned the stool under the light.

The numbers went all the way around the circle, with one small red *x* in the sequence. If those numbers meant anything at all, that must be the beginning. Kip pulled his notebook out of his pack, climbed back on the stool and copied:

2357911131719232931374143475359616771 7379 83899710110310710911 3

That was it. Thank goodness. His neck was starting to hurt with staring upwards.

He climbed down and sat leaning against the window wall. Some watery light fell on the numbers.

What did these numbers mean? Combination lock? Phone numbers? Lottery? Bank machine PINs? Code?

All Kip knew about code-breaking was that *e* was the most common letter in English. What was the most common number in the sequence? He did a tally — 1 was the most common. But so what?

He dropped his notebook. This wasn't his thing. It was Jared's thing. Jared was good at chess and Sudoku and all that brainiac stuff.

E-mail! Of course. E-mail Jared.

Kip rolled his head around. Good. Shelve the mystery and get unpacked.

He put the cot with one end against a wall. He unrolled the sleeping bag. He unzipped the duffle. Mom had packed it. T-shirts, socks and enough underwear for a battalion. All rolled into neat little burritos. He ignored the duffle. The pack was more important. Game Boy, a couple of books, swim mask and fins, a flashlight, CDs and a player. He placed these near the cot. The duffle could go in the closet.

He yanked on the closet door but it was stuck. He tossed the duffle into a corner.

Now all this territory needed was music. He looked around for an outlet for the CD player. He spied one in a dim corner around the side of the closet. He crouched down.

More lace. A different sequence of numbers all around the edge of the outlet. Now he really needed Jared. He copied out that sequence as well.

Something told Kip that there were other numbers in the room, at least one more set. Somehow he knew this would go in threes. He had to find them. It took a while before he thought to look on the narrow edge of the door frame, at right angles to the wall. A different set again. Smaller, neater. Into the notebook.

Looking at the page of numbers, Kip felt a chill creep over him. Writing on walls was fun, of course. Writing on walls was going to be one of the best things this summer. But this was different. So precise, so much work. It was weird.

He suddenly lost interest in claiming his territory. It was too quiet, too solitary, too empty.

He needed some company.

Cousins would do. Locking the door behind him, he slipped the key into his pocket and headed down to the occupied zone.

FOUR

DOWNSTAIRS, the cousins were grouped around a card table. Kip peered between their heads and saw a huge jigsaw puzzle in progress, a border completed and not much more.

He and his mom sometimes did jigsaws, too. They did them quietly. Not so the cousins.

"This picture has way too much green. Bluey-green, yellow-green, greeny-green."

"Are there pieces missing? I'm sure there are pieces missing. Are there pieces on the floor?"

"Pass the box over this way."

"Okay, what I'm looking for is a yellow left-leaning blob garrotted by a blue line."

"Don't jiggle the table!"

"Garrotted? What's that?"

"It's strangling somebody around the neck with, like, a wire or a belt from your bathrobe."

"Remember when we did the map of the world and somebody hid a piece of Mexico?"

"That person, whose name shall not be mentioned, was a deeply wicked person."

"That was so fun."

"That person, whose name shall not be mentioned, deserved to be garrotted."

"Got it! Yellow blob with blue!" Alice banged a piece into place with her fist.

"Hey, listen," said Gran. "What don't I hear?"

"Rain! Come on, let's get to the beach!"

"Hats and sunscreen," Gran called to their retreating backs.

* * *

They set off down the road to the beach like a parade, loaded with towels, umbrella, buckets, Emily's leash, food, drinks, water noodles. Their rhythm band was the music of six pairs of rubber thongs flip-flopping.

Hilary walked beside Kip and did the guided tour.

"That's where Jim the Jaw lives. He used to be in a rock band. He has a jaw like Superman. He used to be a hippie. But now he's old."

Daffodil skipped up beside them.

"Gran used to be a hippie, too. She'll show you the pictures."

"Correction," said Gran. "I wasn't a hippie. I was a free thinker."

"Come on," said Hilary. "Fringed leather vest with beads? Tie-dyed skirt? Photos don't lie."

Between Gran's and Jim the Jaw's, Kip noticed a narrow overgrown trail. That would need to be investigated at some point.

"That's the community hall. They have crafts for sale on the weekends."

"For the tourists," said Alice, in a way that suggested that tourists were lower than slugs.

Hilary continued. "And old movies on Friday nights. Jane, go look at the bulletin board."

"Cats and Dogs," Jane reported.

Hilary groaned. Emily squealed. "Gran! Gran! Pleeeeeeeze..."

"Yes," said Gran.

As they paraded along, cars passed, every one with a wave. Kip's head buzzed with information on who had a backhoe and the feud between the Larsens and the volunteer fire department and how Micah's baby brother could do sign language even though he couldn't talk yet and how now you could buy sushi in the village but there was still nowhere to buy doughnuts.

The cousin chorus swelled with talk about plans for the holiday. Hobo dinner, talent night, trip to the free store, hike to Harraps Point, night swimming, Monopoly marathon. The parade peeled off the road to a path through the woods and emerged onto the beach. Three irregular bands of different colors lay between forest and water. Closest to the ocean was light gray sand, then dark gray flat rocks, then green and yellow scrubby grass.

"Tide's in. Yaaaaay!" The little ones were in the water before Gran had stuck the beach umbrella in the sand.

Kip stopped to help Gran unpack, but she mussed his hair and said, "Oh, go on. Hil and I can manage. Secretly we just want to get to today's crossword." Gran pulled a newspaper out of her bag.

The water was a shock to Kip's toes. He was used to swimming pools. But he couldn't be shamed by a couple of ballerinas and a dog, so he plunged in and churned around like an egg beater until he got over the shock.

Only starvation drove them to beach themselves after an hour of deep sea diving, water-noodle fights, human raft, raise the *Titanic*, synchronized swimming, seaweed hair and Jaws.

* * *

"What are the three types of high clouds?" Daffodil held a cracker in the air. Kip was the only one who even glanced at her. "Cirrus, cirrocumulus, cirrostratus," she announced and popped the cracker into her mouth.

Lunch was full of chewing. Cold wieners, string cheese, peanut butter crackers, plums. And ideas.

Kip was used to quietly swallowing what adults told him. But Gran and the cousins cut up ideas into little bits, ripped them apart, picked one bean out of the chili of a particular topic and held it up to the light to look at in detail.

Jim the Jaw wandered by and was introduced. He winked at Kip.

"A whole month with this lot? You're a brave, brave man."

Then he had a technical discussion with Gran about tent caterpillars before he headed off.

After eating to capacity, the cousins all lay around on the blankets. Gran pulled out the paper.

"Listen to this. This journalist wrote a series of articles about the homeless. She interviewed them and got these wonderful heart-wrenching stories about their lives. She won a prize for the series. Now it turns out that she made it all up. What do you think?"

"Ends and means," said Hilary.

Kip didn't know what Hilary was talking about.

Gran grinned. "Classic ends and means, I'd say. Let's say that these articles made many people more sympathetic to the homeless and in particular caught the attention of some dot com millionaire who decided to give a whole whack of money to build community housing. That's good, right? If the effect of the article was good, who cares if she actually made up the stories? Ends justify means."

It sounded right to Kip.

"That would be good," said Emily. "Homeless people sometimes have dogs and they need houses, too."

"Nope," said Hilary. "Even if that happened it wasn't what the journalist planned. Her goal was to make money and get to be famous."

"Yeah," said Jane. "She was using other people's sad stories just to win a prize for herself."

Gran's eyes were twinkling.

"But we don't know that. Let's give her the benefit of

the doubt. Let's say she really did do it to help the home-less. She thought it was the most effective thing she could do as a journalist. What then? What do you think, Kip?"

Kip felt as though he were bobbing around in deep water with no water noodle. In his experience, when adults said, "What do you think?" as in "What do you think about global warming?" or "What do you think about me getting married?" they usually had a certain answer in mind. But Gran was different.

"I think it would be okay."

"No, no, no." Hilary was practically levitating off the blanket in excitement. "If she really wanted to get the stories of the homeless why didn't she go out and find real people? She's just lazy and a cheat. I mean, the real stories are going to be better than some made-up ones."

"Anyway," said Alice, "if that rich guy finds out the stories are made up, he's going to feel ripped off and probably take his money back."

"There's no way to excuse what she did," said Jane. "It was the same as lying."

There was a small thinking silence and Kip felt himself relax. Of course. They were right. Good. Now he didn't have to worry about it any more.

Gran nodded.

"Hilary raises an interesting question, though. Are real stories necessarily better than made-up stories?"

Aaagh! Kip had had it. Why did Gran want to make everything so difficult?

"I'm going back in. Anyone want to come?"

"Me," said Daffodil and jumped up.

Kip and Daffodil floated around with water noodles under neck and feet.

"I made you up before you came," said Daffodil.

"Made me up? How come?"

"So it could be longer, your visit."

"What was I like, made up?"

"Sleepy."

"Sleepy?"

"Because my mom's uncle, Uncle Nethery, when he wants to go to sleep in the armchair, he says, 'I'm for a kip.' Really I know that Kip, you, is a name and the other kip is just a word, but I sort of pretended you were sleepy. Like Tintin but sleepy."

"Tintin?"

"He's my favorite boy. But your hair's not the same."

On this unarguable truth they lapsed into happy silence. There was laughter from the shore and a small splash near Kip's left ear.

Ends and means, he thought. The means of swimming are floating and moving your arms and legs around. The ends of some swimming are winning an Olympic medal or getting to shore from a sinking ship. But the end of this swimming, right now, is lying on my back, moving up and down with the waves and watching the clouds and the gulls.

Right or wrong?

Neither. Absolutely nothing to discuss.

FIVE

BACK AT GRAN'S, the cousins returned to their projects of deconstruction, decorating and discussion. Gran went into her room and then called to Kip that he had an e-mail.

Gran's computer was old, slow and covered in sticky notes. Kip waited for his message to appear and read the multicolored reminders: Courier = typing. Find Bishop of Partenia. Tidetables.bc.gov.ca. New page = shift, enter.

Gran was hum-singing quietly. "Hum, hum, started to laugh. Hum, humdy, hum, hum, sleep in the bath."

"Gran? Did my dad used to pretend he was somebody else?"

The humming was snipped off. Gran turned to Kip. "What do you mean?"

"That writing on the trapdoor. Drawbridge. I wondered if he used to pretend he was a knight or something."

"Oh, that." Gran sounded relieved. "I think that was just a joke. He did used to…well…think outside the box, go into a world of his own. But he didn't seem to do the usual pretends like knights or superheroes."

The computer made complaining sounds and produced nothing.

"How about you?" said Gran. "Got a made-up self?"

Kip stared at the slowly filling loading bar. Did he? He thought of Daffodil's Kip, a sleepy Tintin with flat hair.

"Not really. When I was in kindergarten I had a Superman cape, but I guess that's just a usual pretend. Ordinary. Boring, I guess."

Gran squished Kip in a hug.

"You must never think that ordinary is boring. The usual pretends are just fine."

Kip glanced sideways at the screen. The loading bar had completely stopped.

"Gran, why don't you get a faster computer?"

"Can't be bothered. Pop and your dad, they were the ones who loved computers. Features, upgrading and all that. I'm just going to keep this one until it gives up the ghost. Oh, look, here comes something. I'll leave you to your message."

The message appeared.

Dear Kipper, We're in the Honolulu Public Library. The minute you get off the plane here everything smells like flowers. Everybody wears flowers, even men. When we arrived at the condo the fridge was broken but Orm fixed it.

We can see hang-gliders from our lanai (balcony). Aloha and love from our island to yours. Miss you, Mom.

P.S. We can get messages here at the library.

Kip hit the Delete button. Was he supposed to reply?

We-talk. He hated that we-talk. Why did everything have to be "we" and "our"? Did marriage make you melt, or what? Forget it. And "Kipper." His baby name. Only Mom called him that. Did she tell Orm? He'd better not try using it.

Anyway, he had a more important message to send. He ran upstairs, grabbed his notebook and returned to the computer. *Hey Math-Head, what do these numbers mean? For your eyes only.* He carefully copied out the long strings of numbers.

Typing strings of numbers was one of life's more boring activities. Kip reminded himself not to become an accountant when he grew up.

* * *

In the living room, Gran looked over her newspaper.

"I got a message from your mom. You, too?"

"Yeah," said Kip. "Orm fixed their fridge."

"Yes," said Gran. "She told me. I sure hope they make it to the leper colony site. I think that must be the most interesting thing in Hawaii." She sank back beneath her newspaper and Kip decided to return to his territory. Out in the hall he saw the sledgehammer propped against the wall. He grabbed it and headed upstairs.

Time to do a little rearranging.

Staring at the closet, he swung the sledgehammer back and forth like a human boy-clock.

Door or wall?

Wall.

The first blow was excellent. The weight of the sledgehammer dug right in. A puff of white dust hung in the air and bits of plaster rained down.

Smash! "Invasion of the Orms." Kip struck a second blow. The hammer stuck and he wrenched it out.

Smash! "One Orm-touch and human flesh dissolves. Earthlings, beware!"

Smash! The head of the hammer disappeared right through into the closet. "Orm-melt. Nation on full alert."

Wrench, smash, smash, smash. "Fridge-fixer, fridge-fixer, fridge-fixer."

Kip rubbed his eyes and coughed. A small pile of rubble lay at his feet and he was covered in fine dust, like the first skiff of dry winter snow. The ragged hole in the wall looked big enough to crawl through.

Kip grabbed the flashlight from his pack and pushed his way through the wall head first, landing with a thump.

Something above him moved and rattled. Kip froze. One minute he wasn't thinking of anything. The next minute his brain was bursting with one thought — Rats.

He pointed his light upwards. Wire coat hangers danced delicately on a rod, tapping gently together.

Kip stood up, pushing the hangers aside, and shone his beam around the closet.

Empty. Nothing hanging. Nothing on the shelf above the rod. Down the slanting wall to the back there was a low shelf. He crouched down.

There was something. On the shelf was a binder.

Kip picked up the binder and backed out of the closet. His eyes were stinging and his throat felt like the Sahara Desert, but the binder demanded his attention.

Black plastic. Three-ring. Kip blew the dust off the cover. A piece of cracked white tape, stuck around the binder like a belt, fell off as he blew, leaving a gritty line of dried glue. He picked up the tape and saw a faint decoration of small black precise numbers. He knew what they would be before he bothered to read them: 2357111...

Invitation or warning? He crouched down and opened to the first looseleaf sheet. A title page. The words were centered exactly.

Confidential Information Regarding Operation Mitochondria

He riffled through the pages. It was a kind of scrapbook. Lists, diagrams, bars of music, faded photocopies, yellowed newspaper clippings stained with brittle tape.

What stopped him were the drawings. Cars, weapons, machines half exposed to show their workings, a camera, a hand constructed of gears and pistons.

They were exactly the kind of drawings that Kip liked. Black and white. Just lines — precise, sure lines that your fingers itched to trace. No smudges or scribbles.

Even the shadows were lines — fine, close, overlapping and perfect. The objects looked real, but more than real.

Oh, to be able to draw like that. Kip had often fantasized that when the genie or magic fish that gave three wishes finally turned up, he was going to use one wish to get the talent to make that kind of picture, to get the edges so right.

But what was it all about?

Kip started again at the beginning. It seemed to be some sort of report.

0900 hours: Operative called to counselor's office. Operative's peers respond with sympathetic noises. Hypothesis: What appears to be sympathy is actually sarcasm.

0904 hours: Operative enters office. Fluorescent lights humming in B flat.

Kip looked up and grinned. He knew what that was about. Perfect pitch. Jared had it. Jared knew what note everything was — cellphone rings, computer warm-up noises, the back-up warnings of trucks. Kip once asked him how he did it but Jared just shrugged. "How do you know green when you see it?"

Back to the document.

0904 hours - 0908 hours: Operative alone in office. Hypothesis: Operative has made another error of Type A: Inappropriate Behavior with Peer Group.

This was weird stuff. The words were like the drawings. Precise, sharp edged, not smudged with adjectives and feelings. It seemed like a science experiment or something, but if you read it slowly you could translate it.

This was obviously a kid in school. And the noises that everyone makes when you get called out of class? That was familiar. It was a kind of "awwww" that went down the scale. The funny thing was that the exact same noise could be friendly or mean. You couldn't describe the difference but you could recognize it. Everyone in the class could recognize it.

What was with the "Operative"? "Inappropriate behavior with peers." Was he a jerk or just out of it? Kip continued reading.

The school counselor did not appear. Instead, two men in suits came into the office. The Operative thought they might be special counselors from the school board or something, and that he was really in trouble for some reason. But then he noticed that they seemed too cool for school people.

Glued to the page at this point were two yellow-edged business cards. One said *J. Stalp* and the other said *L. Hooveman*. No other words. What kind of business card was that? Where was the job title, the phone number, the e-mail address?

Kip looked closer. He realized that although the printing was perfect, the cards were handmade.

It turned out that the Operative wasn't in trouble at all. Instead, the two suits were offering him some kind of off-site educational enrichment program. There was a mysterious but cool conversation, and then the two guys took the Operative away in a car.

The next page was a double-spread pen-and-ink

drawing of a huge car with massive curving fenders and a fierce tooth-like grill. It was drawn from the point of view of someone lying on the ground about a body's length away from the passenger-side front wheel. It loomed. Every detail was there, from the shading on the headlights to the tread pattern on the tires. Kip could almost smell the exhaust and hear the click of the engine cooling.

Tinted-window black sedan. Operative observes that vehicle does not have rear license plate or other form of exterior or interior identifying device.

Yes! This was one of Kip's own thoughts — a car with no words or numbers or logos. He had mentally undressed his mother's car many times, erasing everything, leaving a clean unmarked surface of paint and chrome and fabric. It would be the coolest vehicle. Kip would never have thought of putting this idea into a story.

In a frame under the car drawing was a label. *Vehicle from memory.* Fancy hand lettering.

Kip's stomach did a roller-coaster drop. There they were again, *e*'s with tails.

It was Dad. His binder, his hand, his words, his story. His ghost.

Kip felt his throat tighten. It was like being afraid and eager at the same time. Standing on the edge of a diving board. About to go down and under.

* * *

"Dinner!" A voice from the lower regions floated up. Kip set the binder on the cot. Deep in thoughts of *Operation Mitochondria*, he made his way downstairs.

Gran was draining macaroni in the sink.

"My goodness, you look like the grave-risen. You need a dusting."

Kip glanced down. He had forgotten about the plaster dust.

The ballerinas jumped up.

"Can we dust him? Can we?"

Gran raised her eyebrows at Kip.

"Your call."

"Okay."

The ballerinas gathered rags and a broom, a feather duster and a tea towel and dragged Kip out to the back porch. They tied the tea towel around his eyes and then turned him around three times.

"Why are you turning me around?" said Kip.

"Oh," said Daffodil, "I forgot. You look like you're playing Blind Man's Bluff, so we spun you."

"Really he looks like a terrorist," said Jane.

The mention of terrorism seemed to release something in the duo. The dusting, which had started out gently with the tickly feather duster, became more vigorous, with rags and broom, until it was less like a dusting than a multi-point attack.

Thoroughly dusted and lightly bruised, Kip sat down to dinner. Alice took her macaroni to the top of the ladder. Emily tipped hers into her dog dish. Everyone else behaved more or less normally, although Kip found himself having to expand his definition of normal.

Conversation ricocheted around and Kip floated away.

"Hey, look. Kip's asleep."

Kip fought his way to the surface. "No, I'm not."

"Well, no wonder," said Gran. "He's still in a different time zone."

"Does *everybody* go to bed at seven in Ontario? I'm glad I don't live there."

"Go to bed, Kip," said Gran. "You've had a big day."

Kip stumbled his way to the attic. Teeth unbrushed and unpajama'ed, he fell onto the cot. Half-thoughts struggled with sleep, and lost.

SIX

KIP WOKE UP with sweaty eyelids. Sunlight was blasting through the closed window right onto his head. He sat up and pulled off his T-shirt and socks and lobbed them into the corner. He got out of bed and his feet curled up at the feel of gritty plaster dust on the floor. He tried to open the window wide, but it stuck halfway after one mighty heave.

It was early, but he was wide awake and wondering about the Operative and the Suits. Where were they going in that cool car, and why? You didn't usually get taken to school stuffed in a black unmarked sedan.

Kip was baking hot. Where did that path between Gran's and Jim the Jaw's place go? He picked up the binder.

The kitchen was empty and silent. The whole house was sleeping. Kip grabbed a banana and left by the back door.

Reconnaissance mission.

The path led up a hill. It was overgrown in some places, and one leg brushed against a stinging nettle. A constellation of itchy, painful white dots sprang up. Kip used some inappropriate language and became more alert to the underbrush. After a few minutes the path opened out into a clearing. Long grass and some comfortable-looking logs. A good place for breakfast.

Nobody knows where I am, thought Kip as he opened the binder. It was a good feeling. Is this what it was like for grown-ups all the time? Go where you wanted, the way you wanted? That would be the best thing about being an adult. Well, that and driving.

Back in *Operation Mitochondria*, the Operative got into the car and they set off. The Operative made a list of what was screwy about the situation. Kip nodded as he read.

1. Educators do not typically present business cards to students.

2. Business cards typically contain more information than a single name.

3. Men in question do not exhibit typical educator behavior:

    i. they are too formal

    ii. they are not jovial

4. Stalp and Hooveman do not sound like genuine surnames.

Another star was inked in beside point number four. At the bottom of the page were two small photocopies from what looked like a phone book. Each showed a small red dot. The first dot was between Stalong and Stalsberg. The second was between Hooton and Hoover.

Kip grinned. He hadn't been taken in by that enrichment thing for a minute. Unmarked vehicle. Fake-o names. Who were Stalp and Hooveman, anyway? It had to be a kidnapping. Was the Operative a rich kid?

He flipped back. *Operation Mitochondria.* That sounded like some kind of espionage thing. He hoped so. This was exactly his sort of story.

He ate his banana and continued to read. The Operative had decided to talk to his drivers to gather information. It didn't get him very far.

So, I'm really interested in cars and I figured I knew every current model but I can't figure this one out. Is it European, or what?

Unmoving silence from back of heads. Hooveman: "Limited production model."

That was it for the whole drive. They finally arrived at a district of large, anonymous warehouses. They got in using one of those fingerprint identification systems. They made their way to a small windowless office.

Kip paused and gave his leg a delicious scratch. It really was looking more and more like a kidnapping.

But why was this guy calling himself the Operative? Hey! Maybe he was, like, a bait victim, like those bait cars to catch car thieves. Except, lots of cars were stolen but how many kids were kidnapped out of their high schools? Unless it happened all the time and it was hushed up.

International kidnapping ring? But why? Who wanted high-school kids?

Kip continued to read. First thing in the office one of the Suits took out a knife. After the word "knife," the rest of the page was blank.

Kip turned over in a hurry. No stabbing. The Suit called Stalp just cut off a piece of the Operative's hair. He put the sample into some small machine that looked like a cellphone and read the results on a screen.

Stalp: We need absolute certainty of your identity at the DNA level.

Was this scary or just weird? Kip couldn't tell.

Here the writing ended with a lump and a rusted back end of a staple. Kip turned the page. At the top was a strip of paper printed with something like a blurry bar-code. That would be the DNA reading. Then, stapled to the center of the page was a small plastic zipper bag.

Kip held it up to the light. It contained soft black stuff. Fibers. *Exhibit A: Hair Sample of the Operative.*

This was such a good way to tell a story, with things as well as words. Kip could feel the pleasure of making it all.

The DNA strip was carefully drawn in black ink. And the fibers? What would you use? Wool?

Kip opened the plastic bag. As soon as he touched the soft dryness, he knew. The Operative crashed his way out of the story and stood in front of him.

This was his father's hair. The dark-haired father lying flat in photos was right here, under his fingers.

Kip snatched his hand away as his stomach turned over. He slammed the binder shut. He looked around the sunny clearing.

Where was he? In the story or in the world? Now or ago? At home or away? Himself or outside himself?

Grabbing Dad's hair. Kip was as tall as could be, sitting on his father's shoulders, watching a parade, holding Dad's hair in both hands. A puzzle piece of memory, held in his fingers.

He reached up to push his own hair out of his eyes. Black. Straight. "He's got his dad's hair." Somebody said that, long ago.

A crow landed in front of him and started strutting around in that I'm-the-boss-of-everybody way. Kip's stomach swung back into place. His tongue explored the inside of his teeth and discovered banana and a coating of plaster dust.

A toothbrush called, and some company.

The house was as silent as he had left it. But the sun was quite high. Kip went up the back stairs to the bathroom and de-plastered his teeth. He glanced into Gran's room.

Empty. Family captured by aliens?

Downstairs all became clear as he walked into the living room. Yesterday the girls had never stopped talking but here they were, all of them, including Gran, sitting in the living room in complete silence with their heads bent over empty spools of thread. They were doing things with little picks and balls of wool.

"What are you doing?"

"Good morning, Kip. Spool knitting," said Gran, hardly raising her head. "It's an endangered folk art."

"I'm through, I'm through," said Daffodil.

"Me too," roared Jane.

Both held up their spools. Little worms of woven wool appeared out the bottom.

"Hey," said Emily, "it is sort of like — "

"Never mind what it is like," said Gran. "Some metaphors are best left unspoken."

Kip stood beside Hilary and watched her. Loop and turn, loop and turn.

"Want to try?" said Gran.

"I don't know. What do you do with these…worms?"

"You could call them worms," said Emily, "or you could call them — "

"You sew them together into little round mats," said Gran.

"Or a huge carpet if you make one long enough," said Jane, her fingers flying.

"There's another spool in the sewing box," said Gran. "Help yourself."

Kip flopped down beside Gran and started to paw through her large wicker sewing basket. Scissors in the shape of a bird, thread, a wooden mushroom, an engraved silver thimble in a small leather case, a complicated-looking metal device with neatly moving parts.

"Button-holer," said Gran, "for the sewing machine. Mind you it's a long time since I did button-holes."

The Operative would like that, thought Kip. So cunning and efficient and just exactly engineered for its purpose. He picked up a wooden spool that had four small nails pounded into the top.

"Shall I get you started?" said Gran.

"Okay."

Gran looped the wool onto the nails and showed Kip the technique. It took a little getting used to, but then it was easy. Not an Operative thing, but hypnotic in its way. When the worm popped out the end of the spool he caught Emily's eye. They exchanged a private grin.

His entrance had obviously broken the spell of silence, because the conversation machine kicked into gear again.

"Gran," said Jane, "can I stay up all night, till the dawn's early light?"

"Why?" said Gran.

"I've always wanted to. I hate going to sleep and then waking up and I didn't know what was happening for all that time."

"I love sleeping," said Hilary. "I like everything about it — pajamas, pillows, yawning, dreams, night-lights, being horizontal, the way your toes feel. Sleep is filthy."

"Let me guess," said Gran. "Filthy is good, right?"

"I love everything that is the opposite of that," said Jane.

"There is no such thing as the opposite of pillow," said Daffodil.

"How about a piece of splintery wood with nails sticking out of it?" said Emily.

Or a dream, thought Kip. What's that the opposite of? Waking? Reality? The truth?

"You're welcome to stay awake all night," said Gran.

"But how *can* I?"

"Okay," said Alice, abandoning her spool. "Wait a minute. She roared into the kitchen and came back with the stepladder. She positioned herself next to a blank bit of wall and pulled out her felt pen. "How can Jane stay awake all night? What keeps you awake at night? Gran?"

"My bladder. Getting up three times. Very tiresome."

Alice turned to the wall. "One: pee. Hilary?"

"Nothing."

"Come *on*. You must have been kept awake some-time."

"Oh, yeah. Mosquitoes. Neeeee, neeeeee, neeeeeeee. Right around your ear-holes. Then the noise stops and you know that's because they are biting you. So you try putting the sheet over your head and then you sweat and suffocate."

"Good. Mosquito. Jane?"

"When it's too hot."

"Heat. Emily?"

"Cappuccino."

"But, Emily," said Gran. "Have you ever had cappuccino?"

"No, and I've never had trouble sleeping, either."

Alice continued her list: "Cafeen."

"I said cappuccino," said Emily.

"But I don't know how to spell cappuccino."

"You don't know how to spell caffeine, either," said Hilary.

"Okay, Miss Spelling Queen, whatever. You can figure it out, can't you?"

"Excuse me," said Gran, "is this bickering I hear? I believe there is an anti-bicker order somewhere around here." She peered at the walls.

Alice pulled herself one step farther up the ladder and addressed herself. "So, Alice, what about you?"

"Well, Alice, I can't sleep when I have a cold that plugs up my nose and then I have to breathe through my mouth. In other words…" Alice spun around to the wall and wrote, *Snot*. "Correctly spelled, I believe. Okay, Kip?"

"Worrying." He hadn't meant to say that.

"Worries." Alice wrote it on the wall.

Gran put down her spool and looked at Kip.

"What do you worry about?"

Gran's attention was contagious. Ten cousin eyes turned his way.

"I don't know. Just stuff."

"I hope you're not brooding," said Gran. "Best thing for worries is to talk about them. It is such a bad idea to keep them all inside."

"Yeah!" said Emily. "Just poop 'em out."

Hilary groaned. "Emily, you are wooka gross."

"Well, yes," said Gran. "Emily does have a limited range of metaphors, but in this case she is wooka right."

Hilary rolled her eyes.

"I worry, too." Daffodil didn't look up from her knitting. "I worry just like Kip. I worry about being hit by a meteorite and am I going to get Mrs. Morgan the Gorgon for next year and, like, does Africa really exist."

"Of course Africa exists," said Hilary.

"How do you know?"

"Well, it's obvious. Africa's in atlases. It's on the news. What about all those nature shows? African Safari and all that. Nelson Mandela's from Africa, for pete's sake."

"But it could be all made up. We don't know. We haven't been there."

"Well, we haven't been to Saskatoon, either."

"What makes you so sure that Saskatoon is real?"

"It is real," said Kip. "I flew over it when I came here."

"Ah-ha. Ever heard of holograms?"

"Aaaaaagh." Hilary put her head on the table. "I am trapped on an island with a bunch of schizo nutbars."

"Hilary." Gran spoke very quietly. "I'm not happy with you saying schizo. Even for a pretend insult. It makes light of something too serious."

The jokiness drained out of the room like water down a drain. Hilary sat up abruptly.

"Oh, okay. Sorry, Gran."

Gran shook her head slightly and took a deep breath.

"Do you want to stay up all night tonight, Jane?"

"Yes!"

"In that case, we'll need to make some plans."

* * *

Kip abandoned the brainstorming session about the location of the cappuccino machine and worries about the existence of Saskatoon and went into the kitchen to forage for breakfast.

Over a bowl of cold macaroni and cheese he thought about Gran and her rules. She was hard to figure out. Pee. Snot. Sometimes it seemed as though she would let them do or say anything. But that wasn't it.

That thing about "schizo." She had said the first real rule of the holiday, and Kip knew that nobody, not even Alice, was going to write it on the wall.

SEVEN

THE BINDER looked very ordinary sitting on the cot. Kip pushed plaster debris into a pile with his foot while he stared at it.

Confidential Information Regarding Operation
Mitochondria

It was calling him back. What was going on in that office? Who were Stalp and Hooveman? Good guys or bad guys? And what about the hair?

Oh, come on. Kip shook himself. Get a grip. It was easy to avoid the plastic bag page. The Suits were waiting.

He picked up the binder and opened it carefully.

The Suits told the Operative about a plot, code-named Operation Mitochondria, that some nameless evildoers *("You can appreciate that we cannot be more specific")* were hatching to take over the free world. They were going to infect teenagers with a cell-altering virus. At first it wouldn't seem to make any difference.

However, as the teenagers grew up, when they got old enough to be leaders in whatever — science, politics, sports, research, art — they would just lose it. They would become lazy and stupid.

The plan is, in its way, beautiful. A subtle time bomb. Their promise will flicker and fade. They will lose energy, originality and ambition. Civilization, as we know it, will crumble. It will be vulnerable, like a plum for the picking, to the forces of evil.

The Suits told the Operative that they had reason to believe the evildoers were going to test the plan right there in that very city, and that they needed teenage agents to infiltrate the organization to obtain information. Then they asked the Operative if he would be willing to undertake the assignment. They said it would be dangerous, that they could not guarantee his safety, and that his work could never be publicly acknowledged. He would have to live with the secret his whole life.

Kip paused. One minute you're sitting in class doodling on your eraser and the next minute you're being asked to save the free world. Why would they choose this guy?

You have a suitable genetic imprint. You have an analytical mind. You have minimal status in your peer group. You have a limited number of allegiances.

Minimal status. That would be a loser. Limited allegiances. That would be no friends. Analytical mind. That would be a big brain.

Kip nodded. He knew this person. Smart about math

and computers but with no clue about the ordinary business of friends, school and just being.

Was he going to take the assignment? Kip tortured himself by not turning the page. If it was him, would he do it? Then he grinned. Of course the Operative would say yes. In stories people always say yes and do dangerous things. At least, the hero does. In stories people always go through the forbidden door, or open the forbidden box, or whisper the forbidden secret. Otherwise there's no story, and this was a nice thick binder with lots of story to come.

"Kip! Want to go to the recycling center?" Gran's voice floated up the stairs.

Kip looked at the binder. He wanted to say no. On the other hand, in stories heroes always said yes, and who knew what dragons or mad scientists were hanging out at the recycling center?

The cousins were apparently now all going to participate in the all-night stay-up and they were deep in preparation, so Kip went with Gran alone.

"Hey, look," said Gran as they drove in. "Jim's on glass today."

Jim the Jaw showed Kip the routine, and they spent a satisfying hour hucking bottles and jars into bins. Then Kip and Gran went to investigate the Free Store.

Gran knew everybody and chatted to one and all. She introduced Kip all around. Everyone greeted him as though they knew him. He tried to be polite and friendly but he just wasn't used to so much attention.

He took refuge in shopping and had just scored a 1982 Guinness Book of World Records and a rubber chicken in good condition when Gran called him over to the shoe table.

Sitting in a lawn chair beside the jumbled shoes was a very old wrinkled woman. "This is Vera," said Gran. "She's shoes."

Vera reached up and put her soft hand on Kip's cheek. "Tristan's boy," she said. "Very like, isn't he?"

A little bubble of quiet seemed to enclose them. Gran nodded. Kip saw that her eyes were wet.

"Very like," she said, "but his own fine self as well."

"Tristan and I were great friends," said Vera. "He was a lovely lad. Our hearts were sore, here on the island, when we heard of the terrible accident."

Tristan's boy. Nobody had ever called him that. But that is who he was, here.

Tristan's boy. He was Tristan's boy and Dad was Gran's boy and the accident was not just part of his story but part of Gran's story and the story of this impossibly old person who sorted shoes at the island Free Store.

Kip clutched his rubber chicken and felt his edges start to blur.

* * *

By dinnertime the living room was fully equipped as a stay-awake center. There were extra lamps. An ancient exercise bicycle had been hauled up from the basement. A coffee machine was poised and the screens had been removed from the windows in the hope of encouraging mosquitoes.

Emily was cradling an extra-large bottle of water.

"I'm going to drink a lot so that I have to pee all night."

"You going to stay up?" said Hilary to Kip.

Kip shook his head. "I can't. I'm still lagged. I fall asleep at eight o'clock."

"Awwwwww." Daffodil went up and down the scale a few times. "C'mon. We're going to have so much fun. You'll remember it from now until the rest of your life. Don't worry about falling asleep. We'll keep you awake."

"That's what I'm afraid of."

Jane was already groaning about the slowness of time.

"When's it going to get dark?"

"We could have a story to pass the time," said Gran. "Kip was wondering about the Rootabaga Country. How about the story of the place where the circus clowns are baked?"

"Baked?" said Hilary. "Isn't that very weird?"

"Definitely weird," said Gran. "There is nothing weirder than Rootabaga Country. Anyway, the clowns are baked in ovens. Long lanky ovens for the long lanky clowns..."

"And short squinchy ovens for the short squinchy clowns," said Jane.

"You *know* this story?" said Hilary.

Jane grinned smugly. "Gran told it before. One time when you weren't here."

"Stop interrupting," said Alice.

"I'm not interrupting. I'm participating."

Gran continued. "And when the clowns came out of the ovens, they set them up against the fence in the sun."

"Like big white dolls with red lips," said Jane.

"Then along come two men. The first man throws a bucket of white fire over the clowns and the second man pumps a living red wind into their mouths."

"White fire," said Hilary. "That's filthy."

Gran nodded.

"And they rub their eyes and wiggle their ears..."

"And wriggle their toes."

"And go off and do clown things like cartwheels and handsprings and somersaults and driving around in those little cars with horns that go 'knee-gnaw, knee-gnaw.'"

"The little cars weren't there last time," said Jane.

"No, I added those," said Gran.

"I don't like clowns," said Emily.

"Why not? They are just hobos with make-up."

"They are creepy."

"You like Ronald McDonald okay," said Hilary.

"He's not a clown."

"White face, fat red lips, baggy polka-dot jumpsuit, big floppy shoes? He's as clown as you can get."

"Oh," said Emily. "I just thought he was Ronald McDonald. Okay, I don't like clowns unless they are Ronald McDonald."

"Dinner," said Gran, pulling herself out of the arm-chair.

"Then staying up!" said Jane.

After dinner Kip checked his e-mail and found more news from aloha-land and a reply from Jared.

Hi Tunahead. The first set are prime numbers, the second set is the value of pi, the third set is the square root of two. Hold the applause. Why are you doing math in the summer? Get a life, loser.

Kip grinned. But what was Jared talking about? A little surfing would be a good idea.

Half an hour later, Kip didn't necessarily know much more about math, but his mind was filled with words about numbers.

RAQ (Well, a rare question unless you are a math brainiac.): What is a prime number?

A: A prime number is a number that is divisible only by itself and one.

RAQ: What is pi?

A: Pi is the ratio of the circumference of a circle to its diameter.

RAQ: What is the square root of 2?

A: The square root of two is the number that, multiplied by itself, would give you two.

Only one thing was clear. When you wrote out these numbers as a decimal, each was very, very long. They would go on forever without ever repeating into a pattern. This all seemed very untidy to Kip.

Meanwhile it sounded like the stay-uppers were having a dance party, but the Operative waited in the attic.

Kip settled down with a bag of gummi bears and the binder.

Operative agrees to take on assignment.

Yes! Kip punched the air. As soon as the Operative signed on, he was issued with a weapon. The illustration was beautiful — a detailed, shaded, expanded-projection drawing of a gun, each part separate as though it had been taken apart and laid out on a table, ready to be reassembled.

The Suits told the Operative that the teenagers were going to be infected through a light beam to the retina of the eye. The beam would be introduced using what seemed to be a perfectly ordinary camera. The job of the Operative was twofold. First he was to cleverly attach a eukaryotic neutralizing filter to the camera. Then he was to gather information.

How would the teenagers be persuaded to have their picture taken by a stranger? Graduation photos.

Kip found himself slightly disappointed. Overthrowing the free world using graduation photos seemed a bit…well, silly. He turned the page to find out that the Operative was having the same doubts.

But won't this project take forever? And I don't believe they even have graduation photos in places like Rajathstan.

Of course the Suits had the answer.

There is another element to Operation Mitochondria. In addition to individual genetic modification, the procedure transforms some normal cells into bacteria. Extremely contagious self-replicating bacteria. The altered adolescents become, in effect, sources of a virulent plague. No immediate symptoms. No known effective antibiotic. The plague will spread rapidly, at pandemic speeds, from this specific area to the world population. Only adolescents are susceptible. Global infiltration, via the ripple effect, within twelve months.

Kip distorted a green gummi, then ate it. Yes, that would work. He thought of his school class. Grace went to Hong Kong every summer. One of Jared's brothers was going to travel all the way around the world after graduation. Student exchanges, band trips, family visits. It would all mean spreading the plague worldwide.

There was still a problem, though. The Operation Mitochondria guys, enemies of the free world and all that, were going to get the hero involved in their evil doings, as a way to ensure the school photo contract by offering a work-study incentive. But the Suits got to the Operative first so that he would secretly work for them, the good guys, and use that filter thingo to limit the damage. This was pretty smart because the evildoers wouldn't know for years and years that their plan had failed. The problem was, how did the Suits know that the bad guys were planning to recruit the Operative in the first place?

Kip turned the page to discover that he and the Operative were in sync again.

Hooveman: "Suffice it to say that the operations of Operation Mitochondria are not entirely secure and when you are working with them you will not be alone in the field. Beyond that we cannot say."

Stalp: "You can appreciate that it is safer for you to be in ignorance on certain issues. If you do not know information, you cannot reveal it, even under duress."

Kip decapitated a gummi and gave his stinging nettle itch an absent-minded scratch. So there was going to be another person who would seem like a member of Operation M. but was really working for Stalp and Hooveman. And the Operative wouldn't know who it was. That was going to be good. And "duress." What kind of duress was the Operative going to meet? Garrotting?

Dad was so good at inventing this stuff. High five, dude. There was more discussion of disease and airborne pathogens, but Kip was hoping they would get back to the gun. He flipped ahead a few pages.

There it was. There were more views of the assembled weapon, including an eerie one looking right into the barrel. Kip imagined himself working with the Operative, holding the gun, his hands sliding over the silver-blue metal.

Smooth and secret, sneaky and cool. Pistol-grip stock, ambidextrous thumb safety, adjustable ghost-ring with bar-dot tritium inserts.

Kip sounded out the words and rolled them around in his mouth. They tasted good. Like chocolate. Like power.

EIGHT

EARLY MORNING wake-up again. It was like being five years old. Kip remembered little kid mornings. Boinging awake.

When did boinging turn into clawing your way to the surface? Grade two? Grade three? Why?

Girl-level was silent. The kitchen was empty.

Kip took a bowl of cereal out to the back yard. The grass was wet under his bare feet.

"I don't care for thinning." Gran was kneeling at the edge of the vegetable bed. "Weeding is fine. Begone foul chickweed! But here all these brave beet seeds have done their best and germinated, started to make beets, and here I am, hoicking them out just because there isn't enough room for everybody. Want a carrot?"

Gran wiped the dirt off a little orange finger and handed it to Kip.

Carrots and cornflakes. Not bad.

"You won't see the girls any time soon. They decided

to keep Jane company on her stay-awake. They were still going strong when I bailed out about 2 A.M. They were starting to get grumpy. Whoever was still awake at dawn was likely quite toxic. Have you ever stayed awake all night?"

Kip shook his head. "You?"

Gran dusted her hands together. "Once when we were at university, Pop and I went hiking up in the mountains, and we had this huge fight. We both got so mad we forgot to pay attention to the trail markers and before we knew it, it was dark and we were lost. Idiots. So we had to stay out all night, sitting on a log, eating trail mix and not admitting how scared we were."

"Were there cougars?"

"Cougars was one topic we avoided, if I remember. My other notable overnighter was the day and night your father was born. He was a slowpoke. But that was the last time he was slow at anything. When he was a toddler we called him Mach Two."

"What's that?"

"Mach is the speed of something compared to the speed of sound. Mach Two is twice the speed of sound."

Kip pulled up another carrot. Did Dad move fast? He scoured his mind. He couldn't seem to remember movement at all. Just still images. The Dad he carried with him was getting seriously rearranged. He was becoming a toddler, a Mach Two. He was becoming this new person named Tristan.

"Gran?"

"Yes."

"Why did you choose the name Tristan?"

Gran smiled. "It was all King Arthur's fault. When I was pregnant I came across a book called *Tristan and Iseult*, one of those medieval stories. I sort of fell in love with Tristan. He was one of those giant-killer, dragon-slayer, courageous and clever types. Just the name for a hero baby. And it's Welsh, which my family is, somewhere way back. Later I wasn't so sure about my choice."

"Did he get teased?"

"No, not that. It's just that… Do you take French in school?"

Kip nodded.

"Well, then you know that *triste* is sad in French. I never thought about how I was naming him for something sad."

Gran had stopped weeding. She seemed to have forgotten Kip altogether.

A little insect landed on Kip's arm. He stared at it. Bugs. Bacteria. Self-replicating bacteria. Where did Dad get that cool idea?

"Gran, was Dad ever really sick?"

"Ooph." Gran didn't answer but tipped over backwards onto the grass from her crouch at the edge of the vegetable bed. She seemed to be having trouble getting her breath. Kip helped tip her back.

"Gran! Are you okay?"

"Hand me the hose."

Kip pulled over the hose that was snaking its way

across the lawn. Gran turned on the nozzle and took a drink.

"That's better. How come hose water is the best?"

"But what's wrong, Gran?"

"Oh, it's nothing. I just get a little short of breath at times. Age, I expect. Back to your question, though. What did you mean about Tristan getting sick?"

Gran was acting brisk and Gran-ish, but something wasn't right. Kip wished he had never asked his question, but now he had to continue.

"Just wondered if he ever had, like, a bad bacteria, or the plague or something."

"The plague?" Gran looked over the top of her glasses and gave a crooked smile. "Whatever gave you that idea?"

Kip shrugged.

"Well, there was definitely no plague. Rest assured." Gran handed the hose to Kip. "Care for some Champagne?"

Kip slurped the tooth-numbing cold water.

Gran gave a small groan and rubbed her knees.

"Kip, be a dear and go get me a kneeler from the shed. Green rubber mat thing."

Kip walked to the back of the yard and through the open door of the shed. It was dim and cool, and a sticky spiderweb brushed across his face. He spied the green kneeler on a big cluttered workbench. He grabbed the kneeler, stood in the doorway and did a perfect frisbee toss to Gran.

"Can I look around in here?"

"Go ahead."

Flower pots, rakes, paint tins, a half-bag of cement, tangled lawn chairs, skates, three old doors, a toilet tank, a broken bird bath, jars of nails, ripped window screens, a pegboard of tools, a pile of bricks, bottles of glue, paint thinner, mildew remover, some beaten-up balsa wood airplanes suspended from the ceiling. And that was just the first layer.

In a dark corner, behind two sawhorses, he found a fat bunch of twigs. They were as big around as his thumb and very long, up to the ceiling. He maneuvered them out, knocking over a ladder and taking the skin off one elbow.

Outside he dropped them onto the lawn.

Gran was back weeding.

"Goodness, where did those come from? That shed is such a glory hole of odds and ends. Jim must have put them there. He was on some kick to make twig furniture. It never came to anything."

Kip ran one twig through his fingers. It was smooth, with knobs. It bent without breaking. He whipped it in the air, where it made a delicious slicing sound.

One twig was nothing. Ten was almost nothing. But a huge bundle was something, something in the making. The cousins would all have ideas about what to do with them. The cousins were Mach Two in thinking of ideas. There wouldn't be any room left for his.

"Can I have these?"

"Sure."

"Can I take them to the attic?"

"Go ahead. First step in cleaning out that shed."

Inside the house the coast was still clear, and Kip made the trip upstairs with his long bundles, bending them around corners and knocking pictures askew on the walls. By the time he dropped the last bundle on the attic landing, sweat was running down his face. Spider webs with little gray cocoons clung to his clothes.

He was definitely due for a dusting, but the anti-terrorists were still asleep. A shower might do instead.

After the shower the Operative was waiting. The meeting continued.

Stalp: "Each time we meet you in person our risk of exposure increases exponentially. Therefore such meetings, especially after your training is complete, will be rare. However, you will have our instructions daily. If we need to contact you or you need to contact us…"

Stalp took a plain white piece of paper out of his desk and tore it into rough-edge pieces. He held the two pieces up in the air and slowly, precisely, brought them together. Then he gave one piece to the Operative.

"Unique," he said, "like a snowflake."

"The unique nature of snowflakes is an hypothesis not fully proven," said Hooveman. The Operative noted that the corner of Stalp's mouth twitched.

"If I may continue. You are to keep your half of the paper with you at all times. You may wish to disguise it as a plausible document of some sort. If you receive the matching half

*of the paper you are to immediately abandon the enterprise.
There is no Operation Mitochondria. You never met my
esteemed colleague or myself. In fact we do not exist. Is that
clear?"*

The Operative acknowledged clarity of instructions.

*"For your part, if you are forced to abandon the enter-
prise for any reason, be that suspicion of exposure, serious
threat to personal security etc., then you are instructed to
deposit your half of the paper into an instant teller bank
machine. We will advise you as to the location of this
machine in one of your daily information packages.
Likewise the relevant security number."*

*Hooveman handed a bank card to the Operative. "This
card is designed to self-destruct after a single use. At that
point all the aforementioned history will apply. You never
met us. This place does not exist."*

Kip looked up from the page. Sunlight was moving
across the floor of the attic. From outside came the angry
snarl of Jim's weed-eater.

Bank machine. He had used Mom's card a few times
so he knew the routine. Good idea. After all, there must
be some human who collects all those envelopes that get
sucked in through the slot. Secret operatives infiltrating
banks. Makes sense.

Dad had all these ideas. He must have gone around
looking at the world like he *was* the Operative. All that
boring stuff like bank machines, it could all be more than
it seemed.

Kip and Gran had lunch alone.

"Not a peep out of those overnighters," said Gran. "Shall we go sing something rousing outside their door?"

"Like what?" said Kip.

"How about 'Wake up, Little Susie.' That was one of Tristan's favorites. He used to sing it to you as a lullaby."

"A wake-up song as a lullaby?"

"Well, he was a bit of an eccentric father."

Kip pressed the cheese sandwiches down into the pan. It was his standard Saturday lunch — grilled cheese with the ketchup cooked in and pickles on the side.

Eccentric Dad? Another piece in the Dad puzzle.

What would Saturdays be like with Orm? Would Orm sit with them and eat cheese and ketchup sandwiches? Would Kip make them?

Kip shook his head. No way. Add Orm to the picture and the picture fell apart. Put that in a box and shelve it.

Kip picked up the last crust of his sandwich and chewed it into the shape of a gun. Bar-dot tritium inserts disguised as ketchup. He ate his weapon. Twigs called. He needed to make something.

In the attic Kip spread the twigs out on the floor and ran one through his fingers. Weaving? Possible, but what would you have? A kind of mat or not very strong raft. He held one up and tickled the ceiling. Tap, tap, tap on the light bulb. Scratch, scratch, scratch on the number lace.

He had a memory of watching a hand fit a pole into a ring of holes. It was like a dream memory, definite but not in this world.

Yurts! That was it. The late-night yurt documentary. The finished project flashed before his eyes. A twig yurt, made right inside this room, like a ship in a bottle. He saw himself sitting inside, in the very middle, sitting cross-legged inside a thing he had made.

By the time Kip had lugged tools and nails and a ladder up three flights of stairs, the attic was broiling and the cousins were awake and swarming. When they suggested a beach excursion, it sounded like a good idea to him.

* * *

The water was very calm, as though it was just taking a break between the need to move in and out. Kip floated on his back with the sun beating and dancing on his closed eyelids. The background noise of the up-all-nighters mixed in with the sound of splashing.

"Jane was sleeping."

"I was *not* sleeping. I was just resting my eyes."

"Were too. You didn't even wake up when Emily pretended to be a giant mosquito."

"Hil? Does everybody have to drink coffee when they grow up? I don't want to… It tastes like dirt."

"How do you know what dirt tastes like?"

"I just know."

"Would you rather eat a tablespoon of dirt or a whole jug of coffee? No both, no neither."

"What *is* dirt anyway?"

How could he get the yurt started? Nail the twigs around the bottom of the walls? No, that wouldn't work.

It wouldn't be in a circle. If it was outside you could just dig a circle of holes in the ground, like tent pegs.

Wham! Kip's engineering thoughts were drowned as he was attacked from below and pulled under.

Sputtering, he was pushed to the surface. Jane had his wrists and Daffodil an iron grip on his ankles.

"Let go! I'm not a terrorist!"

"Who cares? You're ours!"

Kip gave one twisting kick and freed himself in a confused splash into deeper water. Through the splashing and laughing he heard a roar.

"Escaped prisoner!"

He flipped over to see Alice sprinting down the beach. He turned toward the distant safety of the raft and began to swim, trying to cut through the water like a knife, but there was no outswimming Alice. She caught him and dragged him into shallow water, to be met by the original attackers plus Emily. One cousin on each limb, he admitted defeat and allowed himself to be floated to shore.

Once on land, the kidnappers decided to bury their prisoner in sand, all except for his head. Alice tried to be the boss but the other three wouldn't let her so she abandoned them, swimming out to the raft. As the remaining trio of kidnappers heaped sand on Kip, they let him in on the story. He was the only grandchild of a billionaire grandmother.

"She's so rich that she has her own plane."

"It's gold."

"And servants do everything."

"They even floss her teeth."

"They even blow her nose."

"Emily! Yuck!"

Emily and Daffodil took turns feeding crackers to the Kip-head lying on the sand while Jane wrote the ransom note demanding three million dollars. Emily took the note in her mouth and delivered it to the rich grand-mother.

Rich-Gran was shocked but she kept her cool. She tried to enlist Hilary as the police but Hilary just pulled her sun visor lower over her face and hid behind her book. After lengthy negotiations the ransom, consisting of half a package of mints, was paid. The kidnappers divided them up fairly. They included the bossy kidnap-per and even the prisoner himself because they were not, after all, really wicked, just very, very greedy.

The prisoner made a powerful escape in a shower of sand and then everyone, young and old, rich and poor, joined him in a final swim.

They dripped all the way home.

NINE

KIP'S YURT revelation came later that night as he was
brushing his teeth. He still had the bottom half to do
when it hit him.

Of course. Drill holes in the floor.

It worked perfectly. He drilled a small but deep hole
right through the linoleum and wood and fitted a twig
into it. It stood, waving slightly like some skinny limb-
less tree. With string and chalk he marked a big circle on
the floor and drilled holes all along the line. Pushing the
fat ends of the twigs into the holes, he made a round
room.

No, not a room. More like a fort. A stockade.

Kip twirled around inside until the twigs blurred into
a wall. He grinned. He had left no door. That was fine.

He snapped off the light and lay down on the cot.
The twigs jiggled in the breeze from the open window.

Tomorrow he would figure out how to join the tops
together. For now the circle was enough. Boy on a cot, in

a stockade, in a room, in a house, on an island. At the center of everything.

* * *

The outer world invaded first thing the next morning. Kip surfaced to the sound of something hitting the outside wall. He was hoping it was a dream sound when it happened again.

Thunk.

He turned over and stared through the softly swaying twigs to the window. A hunk of something appeared, then sank out of sight. There was a chorus of groans from outside, followed by a scornful voice.

"What do you expect? You're not even throwing overhand. Give it here."

Then something flew right in the partly open window. Kip rolled off the cot, reached through the stockade and picked up a piece of paper wrapped around a scrap of wood.

Report to kitchen immediately. Signed: The Beauty Girls.

Kip thought for a moment as he found his pen. He turned over the paper.

Affirmative. Signed: The Male of the Species.

He folded the paper into an airplane and launched it out the window, taking care to remain out of sight.

In the kitchen there was a mysterious Gran-shaped apparition sitting in the middle of the room on a chair. She had a towel around her shoulders, her hands were sitting in bowls of soapy water, she had a plastic bag over her hair and her face was covered in a greenish-brownish gunk except for cucumber slices over her eyes. Her feet were in Hilary's lap, where Hilary was rubbing her heels with a rock.

"We're giving Gran a makeover," said Alice. "Wanna help?"

"Mgphrqg," said Gran.

"Don't talk," said Emily. "You'll crack the mousse."

"What's that on her face?" said Kip.

"Avocado facial," said Daffodil.

"Moisturizes, exfoliates and rejuvenates," said Hilary. "It's wooka stuff."

"Look through those magazines," said Jane. "Gran brought them home from the Free Store. They've got lots of hairstyles. We need to pick one for Gran."

"She's going to let you cut her hair?" Kip was amazed. Bashing down walls was one thing, but was Gran really going to trust the cousins with her one and only head?

"Mgphrpg," said Gran.

"That might mean no," said Hilary. "But at least we can give her a new do."

Gran smelled like food, and Kip found himself hungry. He poured cereal and juice and settled down with a beauty magazine. Daffodil came to sit beside him.

"Nobody in this magazine looks like Gran," she said.

"Well, duh," said Alice. "That's the whole point of a makeover. You get to look like somebody else."

Kip thought that there might be a limit to what you could do with avocado and a rock, but he wasn't about to argue with Alice.

The kitchen timer went off and Alice plucked the cucumber slices off Gran's eyes.

"Can I talk now?" said Gran.

"Sure," said Alice. "How do you feel? Rejuvenated?"

"I feel like a taco," said Gran, "and a bit itchy. I'll just go wash this off."

When Gran reappeared, just a bit green around the edges, everyone launched into a discussion of hair. Emily was in favor of a poodle cut. Alice wanted a purple stripe. Hilary said that a beehive would look wooka blaze.

"Is wooka blaze good?" asked Gran.

"Wooka blaze is uber-good."

Daffodil just wanted something pretty, and Gran voted for no change at all.

"Gran!" Alice was very stern. "How long have you had that hairstyle?"

"Well, I don't even think of it as a style, actually, but it has been the same since about 1975."

Alice shook her head sadly.

"Maybe you could put in some rollers," said Gran weakly.

Alice didn't even bother to reply.

Finally, after much discussion, everyone went with Kip's suggestion, which was gel. It was dramatic, it was temporary and, most of all, Hilary had some.

Everybody enjoyed the gelling, but they couldn't quite get the gelled bits to stand up right.

"I know," said Kip. "Get the vacuum. And be sure to bring the crevice tool."

Kip felt the respect level in the room rise considerably.

"Wow," said Daffodil. "How do you know that?"

"Halloween," said Kip. "Jared and I went as the Evil Hedgehogs of Doom. Vacuuming with the crevice tool was the only way we could get the right effect."

It worked perfectly. Soon Gran's hair stood up in very satisfactory stiff points, and they were all ready for the moment of truth. Hilary brought in a mirror. Gran took a careful look and declared that she felt like an entirely new woman and was looking forward to exploring her inner sea urchin, but that just at the moment she needed a moisturizing and rejuvenating cup of tea.

* * *

Confident after one successful project, Kip tackled his yurt problem after lunch. But everything fell apart. He tried to attach the twig ends to a center point in the ceiling but nothing worked. Glue, string, wire, hooks — the whole thing was just too floppy. Each try was less neat, less right, less satisfying than the last. The twigs were fighting him.

He lay on his back on the floor and glared at them.

"Okay, you suckers, I'm just going to nail you to the ceiling."

Scrambling through Pop's jars of nails, he found what seemed the perfect thing. U-shaped nails with two pointed ends. He put a handful on top of the ladder along with the hammer. Then he grabbed the waving end of a twig and climbed up. Wedging himself between ladder step and ceiling, he picked up the hammer and a nail. He gave a big swing.

The hammer glanced off the nail and hit Kip's thumb, hard. Kip yelled and dropped the hammer, which bounced off the ladder and sent the nails flying. Kip jumped/fell off the ladder, scraping his leg on the metal edge of the cot on the way down.

Then he cried. He cried for the pain in his thumb and the pain in his leg. He cried because there was nobody to be mad at except himself. He cried because he hated crying.

Then, scraping his sleeve across his leaking eyes, he got up, pushed through the stockade, opened the trapdoor and thumped down the stairs to the bathroom.

The door was closed, and from inside came the noise of a hairdryer. Girls!

He thumped down to the main floor and used the toilet there. When he came out, he heard kitchen sounds of talk and giggling. Girls! He slammed the bathroom door.

"Kip? There's an e-mail for you." It was some cousin or other.

Forget it. An e-mail from happy hula-land was the last thing he needed. He yanked open the front door and left. Let them worry if they wanted.

The day was overcast. The sky was just holding its breath before it began to rain. The beach was deserted. The tide was out.

Kip walked along the high tide line, kicking driftwood and crunching shells. He inspected his leg, hoping to see blood, but there was only a faint red mark. He picked dried glue off his fingers and gave his thumb a gentle, painful squeeze. A crowd of tiny fast-running birds whirred along the water's edge and took off in a cloud. Kip tried not to let them make him feel better. He gathered some stones and pitched them out to sea, blasting over home plate, burning a hole in the catcher's mitt. He settled his feet more firmly in the sand, curling his toes in its cold grit.

Strrrrrike! Strrrrrike! Out!

The beach ended in a pile of barnacle-encrusted rocks. Climb up? Maybe not. He didn't want keelhauled feet. The rocks made a little half-cave, a cave without a ceiling.

Kip crawled in.

Wood, seaweed, smooth sea glass and sharp broken shells.

Something white and different poked out from under the driftwood. Kip extracted it.

It was a styrofoam life preserver, a bit chipped and grotty with sand, but in one piece. Kip brushed it off and put it over his head. It slid down to his waist.

Had somebody been preserved in it? Was that how it got to shore?

He felt something sharp poking into his waist. A bit of shell had become embedded in the styrofoam. Kip pulled it out and the yurt solution came to him.

This was what he needed. A gift from the sea.

Back in the attic, the life preserver worked perfectly. Kip attached it to the ceiling around the light, using leather strapping he found in the shed. Then he poked the free ends of the twigs into glue and then into the sides of the styrofoam doughnut.

Dip, pop and push. It was delicious. He had found the one perfect way among all those messy, muddled, wrong ways. Kip the Impaler, he said to himself with a grin.

When the structure was complete, Kip admired it from all angles, inside and out. Part of him wanted to show it off. But another part was not ready for an infiltration of cousins. No, right now he only wanted to invite one person in.

The Operative. The Operative would see that it was smart and solitary and cool. The Operative would sketch it and call it something like a Base of Maneuvers.

Kip dug out the binder and a granola bar and lay on his cot. He opened to a lumpy page. There was a bank machine card with the name sanded off, held in place with photo corners.

Basic training was obviously over and the communications network had been set up. Now it was time for some action.

Kip was ready to meet the evil-doers. He played a tiny suspense-inducing torture game with himself by flipping forward in the binder. He didn't let himself read anything. He just looked at what was coming.

There were more diagrams. There was a page of

graphs. "Velocity of Optimum Angle" and "Arc of Tolerance." Kip liked their neat patterns. They would make great T-shirt designs. It wasn't exactly like reading a book, all put together and tidied up. It was a bit like a video game because you could just jump around and you had to piece together the story yourself. But there were no scornful blooper sounds or dings of triumph. There was no score, no way of knowing if you were right.

He paused at a page of sayings:

I am a singularity and duty is my greatest gift.

Pare down.

Hone the edge.

My needs are less than dandelion fluff blown in the wind.

The next page had little squares of fabric stapled to it. They had words printed or embroidered on them: *Rivershirt. Bentley Bros. Jerboa Co. Re*Flex. Denarius.* At the bottom was a paper flap. Kip opened it. *Beware Labels. They Are a Portal.*

Then there was more gun information:

Your weapon is completely silent and adaptable to self-defense should all other systems fail. Its ray-neutralizing capacity can convert, in a series of manipulations known only to the Operative, to Infarct Mode — an instant, bloodless, undetectable source of heart failure.

This was amazing. The weapon could cause a heart attack, and nobody would think to investigate. It was the ultimate assassination weapon.

What followed was a series of diagrams of the gun,

converting, step by step, from one function to another. The best Transformer.

Finally the Operative got back to the story, sort of. It began confusingly with a small brown mark bordered by a box and then a list of injuries.

Cut lip
Abrasions to right arm
Black eye
Bruised ribs

Following the list was a report on an attack on the Operative. Kip figured out that three guys had jumped him in an alley. As usual, the Operative's report was plain:

Accusations include:
1. being a weirdo
2. being a creep
3. thinking I am somebody cool

But Kip knew exactly what it had really been like. There wasn't a boy alive who wouldn't know that. They would come at you, pretend-friendly. "Hey, Mister Creep-Face, how's it going?" Then they would ask the same question over and over, each time getting a little closer.

"Where you goin'?"

"Where you goin', huh?"

"Where do you think you're goin'?"

Silence or speech. Each was worse than the other.

"What did you say? We can't hear you. Speak up, Mister Creep-Face. Where did you say you were going?"

There would be a poke in the arm. A light little thing, almost friendly. Then a shove. Then you were down.

Fight back or try to escape or put your arms around your head and give up. Each was worse than the other.

Then everything was kicks and punches and laughter and snot and no air and no end and the pain you knew was coming.

Kip found himself breathing shallowly just thinking about it. The Operative dissolved for a moment, leaving Dad in his place. Tristan Coulter knew about this stuff. Did it happen to him?

Kip heard cousin noise downstairs. Maybe he didn't want to read any more right now.

But, glancing forward, he saw that the report changed.

Unmarked black car, limited production model, attends scene. Three men in suits emerge. Extract small silver guns. Hold them lightly as they approach attackers. Attackers attempt escape but Suits flick out their arms and secure attackers. They inflict invisible pain. Suits speak. Their voices are low and polite. "You were never here. This never happened. We do not exist. You do not know this boy. You will never speak of this." After each statement they ask, "Understood?" and the attackers twitch and moan with pain until they nod.

Kip exhaled. Those Suits were so cool. Without moving a muscle. They didn't even appear to try. Sometimes — just some rare times — he felt like that. Diving without a ripple, skating to a stop in a shower of ice just a snick from the boards, understanding something hard.

To feel like that every minute, that smooth rightness — that is what the superhero thing was all about.

Suddenly there was a thumping on the floor under Kip. He started with surprise. A weird muffled voice called out, "Planning meeting. Planning meeting. All hands on deck." Bang, bang, bang.

Kip watched the yurt vibrate with each thump. He sighed. The cousins were massing outside the stockade.

TEN

THE KITCHEN was full of steam and girls. The Sea Urchin of Doom was boiling a big pot of water for corn.

"I told you," said Alice from atop her ladder. "He's got to be building a climbing wall. I tried that but the holes just kept crumbling."

"Nope," said Hilary. "He's making a den of iniquity."

"No fair," said Emily. "I want a den of iniquity, too."

"Do I hear whining?" said Gran.

"You don't even know what a den of iniquity is," said Alice.

"Do, too. It's like a doghouse."

Kip fingered the key hanging around his neck.

"Kip will reveal all when he's ready," said Gran. "Meanwhile, we've got some things to plan." She plunked a big bowl of corn on the table.

For a brief moment nobody talked except Daffodil, who quietly recited the names of the flat and sharp keys in music while she rolled her corn in butter.

"Right, then," said Gran. "I call for the vote. Which comes first? Hobo dinner or talent night?"

"Hang on," said Hilary. "Kip doesn't know what he's voting for."

The vote hung in the balance as Hilary explained the nature of the two events so that Kip could be an informed voter. Kip voted for the hobo dinner with all his heart. He was hoping they could delay the talent night indefinitely.

Kip didn't have a talent. Talent was like Jared writing his own computer programs. Talent was when that new kid, Ming, did that amazing gymnastics routine in the school playground on her first day and shifted power away from Sondria, the girl dictator of grade five. Talent was Dad drawing a car so real you could hear it. Talent was ribbons and trophies and certificates and marks.

"A talent for helpfulness." That was what his grade one teacher had written on his report card. Great. Maybe he could clean blackboard erasers or pass out little containers of arithmetic macaroni.

The hobo dinner support team, meanwhile, was cheering in triumph and planning for the very next day.

* * *

The next morning Kip was itching to get back to yurt life, but Gran insisted on a beach hike.

"Come on. Let's get some fresh air. The weather is gorgeous."

There were moans all around.

"Gran thinks we won't grow up right if we stay inside too much," said Hilary. "She thinks we'll grow up to be unemployed misfits with bad posture."

"Yeah, and zits," said Alice.

"And dandruff?" said Daffodil.

"Yup, dandruff," said Jane.

"And dog breath," said Emily. "But I wouldn't mind."

"You're absolutely right," said Gran. "See what I'm saving you from? Get your hats. We're off."

The hike started from the swimming beach and carried on around a rocky point. Emily attached her leash to her collar and handed the other end to Kip.

"You're my human."

"He's my human, too," said Daffodil.

"Yeah," said Jane. "He's not just Emily's human."

"You don't need humans," said Alice. "You *are* humans."

Hilary started to sing something about people who need people, and Jane pointed out highlights.

"That's the bouncy log."

"Three generations of family bounces," said Gran.

There was a rock shaped like a creampuff and the eagle's nest and the dangerous cliff in the distance.

"It's the only good rock-climbing wall on the island," said Alice in a tragic voice. "And Gran won't let us climb it."

"You have to wait until you've had a climbing lesson and you have proper gear," said Gran. "Ropes and things. Then you can give it a try."

"Wait, wait, wait. That's the story of my life."

The beach got rockier and rockier.

"Freedom for dogs," said Gran. "Come on, Emily, unhook yourself. This is the leash-free zone."

The leash-free Emily raced on ahead, dancing across the rocks with Alice, Jane and Daffodil. Kip walked beside Gran and Hilary.

"Should we get her one of those quick-release collars?" said Gran. "I'm a bit worried that she'll get caught on something."

"I don't know," said Hilary. "Isn't it a bit weird that we all go along with this dog thing anyway? At home she doesn't get to eat out of a dog dish."

Gran shrugged. "Grandmother's privilege to let dogs be dogs, I guess."

Hilary grinned. "You're just a softie."

Kip wandered down to the water's edge. He looked back at Hilary and Gran. They never stopped talking. Hilary stayed close to Gran, putting out a hand to steady her.

Hilary was hard to figure out. How old was she, anyway? Going into grade ten, she'd said. Fifteen, probably. A kind of grown-up. She always seemed to know what was going on and what to do about it. She never seemed to be trying to figure things out.

Kip sometimes felt like his life was one whole brain-aerobics exercise in figuring things out. It was like looking out through a screen door. You could see what was out there but it wasn't very clear. Did you get it sorted by fifteen?

The hike slowed down almost to a halt as the cousins peered under rocks. Jane knew the names of all the creatures. Hermit crabs, sea stars ("Not starfish, they're not fish"), anemones, sea slugs. Kip shifted a rock and looked into a small wet cave. Stuck to the wall was a bright white sausage with brilliant orange pimples. It looked sort of disgusting, but if the cousins weren't doing that "eee-yuck" thing, he sure wasn't going to.

"Orange-spotted nudibranch," said Jane.

Kip glanced down the beach and then back into the cave. From a distance the beach looked mainly gray, but close up and underneath it was so fancy. The Suits would like that. Gray and plain on the outside but complicated, surprising and slightly disgusting when you investigated further.

Alice spied some seals heaving themselves up onto rocks out in the bay. The humans found their own rocky viewing spots and settled down to watch. Three big seals claimed one rock and got cozy, curling their tails up and shifting around. Two smaller loners found rocks of their own. The sixth seal swam around and around, black head appearing and disappearing. He came up close to three-seal rock and a great barking and growling erupted. Then he tried the loners, but they were just as unwelcoming.

"Poor seal," said Daffodil. "Nobody likes him."

The Sixth Seal, thought Kip. That would be a good code name for an espionage operation.

"Ki-ip?" said Emily, with a sweet little smile.

"Oh, boy," said Hilary. "Here we go again."

"What?" said Kip.

Emily's eyes grew wide with innocence. "Do you know what the French word for seal is?"

"Emily," said Gran, "we've all had enough of that joke, thank you."

"I'm very good at French," said Emily. "Because I'm so oral."

A ship's horn sounded and the sextet of seals disappeared.

"That's the four o'clock ferry," said Gran. "Time to be heading back."

* * *

Gran declared the late afternoon to be down time, and Kip went up to his territory. The yurt was even better than he remembered. Inside it seemed like a real place. A place for himself and the Operative.

The Operative did not mention the attack in the alley again but had gone back to a description of weapons — explosives this time.

Device WF/RW* fulfills the essential requirements for use in the project.

1. Miniaturization: Dimensions 6x2x1 cm.

Kip held up his finger. Okay. Size of an eraser.

2. Precision. Tolerance of one micron.

3. Universal interruption-immune remote detonation control.

4. Self-repairing capacity.

*White Fire/Red Wind.

White fire and red wind. That was familiar. Had the Operative already used that phrase?

No. It was from Rootabaga Country.

Gran. Baked clowns leaning against the fence, made-up things brought to life. How come the Operative…?

Kip pulled himself out of the story, like pulling himself out of water. Gran must have told that clown story to Dad when he was a kid. Two men, one pouring white fire, one pumping red wind. Then he put it in his own story.

Fire and wind and coming alive. Gran and stories and Dad and stories, all mixed in together in this plain black binder. Kip felt a bit hollow.

* * *

The family sat in the flickering light of the dying campfire, and Gran handed out cigarettes.

Alice took a deep drag and held hers out at arm's length.

"The life of a hobo is the life for me," she said.

"I had a terrible time finding cigarettes this year," said Gran. "Had to ask Jim to pick them up on the mainland." She peered at the package. "And, look, they don't even call them cigarettes. They call them fun tubes."

"Well, I guess," said Hilary. "Talk about a janky role model. Candy cigarettes."

"But we have to have cigarettes," said Jane. "We always have them after the hobo dinner."

Kip bit the pink end off his fun tube. Wieners and

beans heated up over a campfire in the back yard, eaten off foil plates. Everyone dressed in patched clothes and bashed-in old hats from the dress-up box in the basement.

Kip looked across the fire. Disapproving or not, Hilary was playing the smoking game for all it was worth. She held the cigarette between thumb and index finger, tapping the end with her pinkie. Then she narrowed her eyes and tossed her hair.

"You call this dump a hotel?"

Gran inhaled her coffee, laughing, coughing and spluttering.

"You're supposed to be a hobo, not a glamor girl. Where do you get this?"

Jane groaned. "It's all those boring black-and-white videos she watches."

Hilary held her cigarette like a pointer aimed at Kip.

"He's as shifty as smoke, but I love him."

The smalls went into convulsions.

"He's blushing, he's blushing."

Kip covered his face with his hands and wished for a girl-less world. Shift and enter! Shift and enter! Blank page right now! Alter cousins, or better yet, DELETE!

He started to get up but Alice launched herself across his legs and held him pinned down.

Like everyone, Alice was dressed in layers, an old plaid shirt over a limp gray tank top. But there was something odd about the plaid layer — a neatly cut square hole just below the collar.

"There's a hole in your shirt," said Kip.

"Of course," said Alice. "I'm a hobo."

"No, it's not that kind of hole. Look at it."

Alice sat up, slipped off the shirt and put her eye to the small window.

"Oh," said Gran, "I didn't know there were any of Tristan's old shirts still around."

"It was my dad's?"

"Yes," said Gran. "From a time when he cut all the words out of his clothes."

"Why?"

"Oh, I don't know," said Gran. "He had some funny ideas."

"Protesting the logo-driven power of multinational corporations and the exploitation of garment workers in the Third World?" said Hilary.

"I don't think so," said Gran. Her voice was flat, with no laughing in it.

Hilary looked startled.

"Hey, Gran. Is something wrong?"

"No, no. I'm just a bit tired." Gran sat back in her beach chair and her face fell into shadow.

Kip felt a little nudge of memory. *Beware Labels. They Are a Portal.*

Dad had been acting out Operation Mitochondria. And Gran didn't know about that. He, Kip, was the only person who knew.

"Can I switch shirts with you?"

"Sure." Alice slipped off the shirt and handed it to Kip.

He pulled it on and buttoned it right up to the neck. The flannel was soft and thin. He was himself and his father.

He was shifty as smoke.

ELEVEN

KIP WAS LYING in a perfect balance of three water noodles when it hit him. He shifted with his thought, and one water noodle went springing out from beneath his knees and leaped into the air. The other noodles took the opportunity to make their own break for freedom, and Kip got dumped upside down. A noseful of seawater. He coughed and sputtered into shore, abandoning the treacherous noodles, and lay in the shallows. The thought was still demanding attention.

He reviewed recent events in Mitochondria. The Operative was busy decoding junk mail. The Suits were feeding him instructions via unsolicited mail delivered through the door. Real estate ads, discount coupons, pizza flyers. It was all cleverly encoded information. Letters and numbers were circled, and there were charts with number/letter grids. Kip couldn't figure any of it out, but he liked it. There was one, a drawing of a poodle from a dog-walking service flyer, which was superimposed on a map of some city. The poodle's nose, which covered a particular street intersection, was marked with a small red dot.

Once you started thinking like the Operative, it all made strange sense. But — and here was the thought that had dumped Kip in the water — something didn't add up with Stalp and Hooveman. Did they rescue the Operative from that attack in the alley? But how did they know what was happening? Was the Operative under surveillance? Why? Or were the rescuers the evil-doers of Operation Mitochondria? Had the Operative blown his cover? Who was trying to intimidate him, and why?

Kip slapped his hands down on the water. What about if O.M. and the Suits were the same thing? What about if O.M. didn't exist, was just a front? What about if the grad photos were just…grad photos? What about if O.M. and the Suits were *all* the enemy who wanted the Operative for a completely different reason?

Dripping, Kip headed back to the house, to the attic, to the inside of the Operative's mind. He wrapped Dad's flannel shirt around him.

Bingo! They were on the same wavelength as usual. Kip grinned. Mind meld.

The Operative had had Kip's exact doubts about his fortunate rescue. He, too, wondered who had known about that attack.

As for the question of how, he had a very ingenious idea.

Comprehensive body survey to locate position of tracking device.

Tracking device? Kip remembered this book he had read for a project on endangered animals. Scientists capture wolves, polar bears, giant turtles, and insert little radio transmitters under their skin to track their movements. The Operative must think that somebody had done that to him.

Human tagging. Kip felt a shiver flash through him. He flipped the page.

Two outlines of a human body, front and back, were marked with tiny numbers. A numerical list on the side of the page was annotated. *Freckle, freckle, scar, freckle, scab, freckle, freckle, freckle.* Number 27, *White dot left thumbnail,* had a red star next to it, and a note. *Probable location. Defect not previously noted. Monitor.*

Kip looked down at his own fingers. He had three of those dots on his own nails. Were they there last week? Who knew?

The Operative was right. It would be a subtle way to implant a device.

The next page contained only three words, neatly printed in the exact center, *Knowledge Is Power.*

Kip grinned. The Operative now knew something the evil ones (whoever they turned out to be) didn't know he knew. That gave him the upper hand. How would he use this power?

Current Report: Operation Mitochondria Neutralization progressing as planned. Three high schools completed.

Retinal weapons reliably disabled. Operative has mastered cultural norms camouflage. Example: buying doughnuts and contributing to on-going jovial atmosphere.

Cultural norms camouflage. Kip knew what the Operative was talking about. So much of being in the world seemed like that. You put on your camo clothing and figured out how to blend, to fit in. You paid attention and figured out when to speak and when to remain silent. You figured out when to laugh and when to buy doughnuts.

He turned the page.

Surveillance Test: Use silver thumb device to block transmission signal. Goal: To provoke agents or counter-agents into communicating with the Operative.

A diagram followed of an open case into which was fitted a small cup decorated with a delicate wave design.

Kip stared. He put down the binder and ran downstairs. Gran's sewing basket was still sitting beside the couch. He rummaged around in it. Five abandoned spool-knitting projects and the bird scissors and a silver thimble in a leather case.

He flipped open the tiny clasp. In a nest of faded blue satin sat nestled a perfect wave-decorated laser-blocking device, to confuse the forces of evil, to force them to reveal their true identities, to save the free world.

Kip fitted the thimble over his thumb. It may have blocked the transmitter rays to S&H, but it was transmitting loud and clear to him.

It was another meeting with his father. A teenager. A

smart teenager with lots of freckles and two scars and not many friends. A teenager who liked espionage and numbers and tools that were beautiful, like his mother's thimble. A teenager who had a movie running in his head all the time.

And the only other person sitting in that movie theater, eating the popcorn, following the spies, peering down the dark alleys, examining the weapons, was Kip.

* * *

The evening had been declared talent night. There was no stopping the force of tradition. Kip spent the afternoon in serious avoidance. He read several faded Peanuts comics and the eating section of the world records book. He had a triumphant run with the puzzle and finished the whole orange section. He retrieved and even answered his mother's e-mail saying, yes, that he guessed the luau must have been fun. He did a Google search for the French word for seal. He said it aloud and grinned. Finally he collapsed in front of the TV and tuned in the soaps.

Meanwhile, all around him concert preparation raged. Guitar music, ballerinas en pointe, furniture moving and something that sounded like a dog singing a lullaby.

"What are you going to do tonight, Kip?" Daffodil stood between him and The Tough and the Tender.

"I'm going to be helpful," said Kip. "I have a talent for helpfulness."

"Oh, I thought you might show us what you're making in the attic."

"No, it's not that good or anything."

"Oh." Daffodil didn't move.

"And it's not really finished."

Daffodil nodded. "The Robertson's the one with the square tip. The Phillips is a cross."

"What?"

"Screwdrivers. Two kinds. The Robertson was invented by a Canadian. I know how to use them both. And flat-head, of course."

Some Tough and/or Tender was beginning to sob. Kip slid down the couch so he could see the screen.

"Just so you know," said Daffodil.

"Hmm."

In a couple of minutes Daffodil wandered off. Later Kip muted for an ad.

Robertson and Phillips. Daffodil and her facts. Then he heard her voice as in an echo. "Just so you know." There had been something disappointed in it.

Oh. Daffodil had been offering to help with Kip's project. And he hadn't even answered her.

"He's adopted, just like me."

"I made you up before you came."

Of all the cousins Daffodil was the one who sometimes couldn't keep up, who often didn't know what was going on. Like him, Daffodil often didn't know the means or even the ends. He would pay her more attention.

And what about tonight? Maybe he should just do it, take everyone up to the attic for a tour of the yurt. But talent night was obviously a performance thing. Besides, if the cousins saw the yurt, they would cover it with talk and girl molecules, and then it wouldn't really belong to him — to him and the Operative.

The Operative! Kip straightened up on the couch.

That was it, the answer to the concert.

TWELVE

IN THE LAST-MINUTE preparation for talent night, Kip was very helpful. He moved furniture, rolled up the rug and played around with extension cords to create theatrical lighting. He made a paper crown for the rubber chicken and positioned her front row center.

The cousins went upstairs to change clothes and giggle, and Gran stood on a step stool and wrote on the wall beside the stage area.

Stars of Tomorrow

Act One
Musical Offering by Hilary
The Amazing Dog Show
Kip's Mystery Act
Intermission (ice cream will be served)
Act Two
Informative Lecture on Rope Climbing
Ode to Terpsichore

Daffodil and Jane ran into the room trailing wispy scarves behind them.

"Where's us?"

"You're Terpsichore," said Gran. "Terpsichore is one of the nine muses, the muse of dancing."

"Are the nine muses useful facts?" said Daffodil.

"I guess they are," said Gran. "They come in very handy for crossword puzzles."

Dinner was pizza off paper plates so that the talents could begin as soon as possible. The audience settled in and Hilary stepped onto the stage with her guitar.

"Ladies, gentleman and chickens."

She performed in her hobo clothes. To start she played guitar and sang a funny song about the hobo life. There were mountains of candy and rivers of lemonade and the cigarettes grew on trees. Hilary's voice wrapped itself around them all — easy, big and clear. Then, with no guitar, she sang a song in another language, with a tune that you couldn't predict at all. It was so strange and sad that Kip forgot all about his coming performance.

"That was just lovely," said Gran. "I don't know where you get this musical gift. Sure isn't from me. Voice like a frog, tin ear and fumble fingers for all instruments. And Pop was the same. He told me once that his hopeful parents persisted in him taking violin lessons for seven years! Can you believe it? Nobody was willing to face the obvious and painful truth. Then I end up with a musical son. He would spend hours figuring out complicated chord changes on the piano. And then a musical granddaughter. It seems that talent moves like a knight in chess, across and down rather then straight down. Anyway, enough talk, what's next?"

To nobody's surprise, Emily's performance involved sitting up, begging for a treat, rolling over and fetching. For her grand finale she dived through a hula hoop onto the air mattress, and then bark-sang to a collection of Raffi songs.

Her act was long, but not nearly long enough for Kip. As she barked an encore, he rolled up the soft sleeves of Dad's shirt and opened his journal.

"Ah," said Gran, "something from the literary arts."

Kip looked down at his own messy handwriting. He looked out at the audience. Jane and Daffodil curled on the couch, Alice cross-legged on the floor, Hilary stroking Emily's head, Gran leaning against the wall with her mug of tea. His new-found family.

He picked his words carefully.

"This is something I wrote out." He cleared his throat. "Diary of an Operative. The forces of darkness are everywhere, massing at the gates of freedom. Security is an illusion. Complacency is our enemy. Operative carries out an inventory of domestic access points. One: telephone answering device, screen for microphones. Two: television, screen for surveillance cameras. Three: electric outlets, screen for sub-atomic rays. Four: hot air registers, screen for nerve gas. Five: unsolicited mail, screen for embedded instructions, double screen for enemy infiltration by Operation Mitochondria — "

Gran interrupted. Her voice was harsh and odd. Kip couldn't catch what she said.

"Yes, Gran?"

"What did you say just then?"

"I'm lost," said Jane. "What's unsolicited mean?"

"You know," said Kip. "Junk mail."

There was a gurgle from the corner. Kip looked back at Gran in time to see her open her mouth and then suddenly drop her mug, grab her chest and start to slither down the wall. There was a thump as she disappeared behind the couch.

"Gran!" Hilary jumped out of her chair.

Kip dropped his book and ran over. Gran lay in a heap. She was breathing in fast little breaths. There was a clamor of cousin voices out of which he heard, "Dial 911."

He found the phone. In the long, long pause between one ring and the next, he found and lost Gran's address in his head.

"Emergency services. Police, fire or ambulance."

His brain was crawling slow. Not police. Not fire.

"Ambulance."

"I'm connecting you now."

1436 or 1346? Kip couldn't remember.

"Ambulance services."

"My gran. She's sick."

"Dispatching an ambulance to 1436 Straitsview. Correct?"

They knew already. "Er…yes."

"Please stay on the line. Is the victim conscious?"

"Just a minute." Kip handed the phone to Hilary.

Gran was lying with her head on a pillow. Her face was gray and wet. She was talking in little gasps.

"No need…for a fuss. I'll be…fine."

Kip knelt down in the spilled tea and took her hand. Hilary was still on the phone.

"Yes. Just fell over. Yes, she's talking but she's not talking right. I don't know. Sixty or something. Old. My grandmother, yes. Fourteen. No, just us. I'm the oldest." Hilary held the phone away from her ear. "Gran, the ambulance is coming."

Kip could not tell if Gran understood. She was moving her head in little shakes.

The little ones were huddled together. Daffodil had her thumb in her mouth. Their eyes were huge and they weren't saying a word.

Gran's hand suddenly squeezed Kip's. "Get…get Jim."

Kip leapt to the door. "Getting Jim."

Hilary nodded and the little ones shifted.

Kip banged on Jim's door. The house echoed a message of emptiness. He jumped off the porch and around the side.

Get Jim. Where was he? There. At the far end of the garden, levering up weeds.

"Jim!" Kip's voice was a frog croak on two different notes. But Jim heard, turned, dropped his tools and crossed the lawn with long strides.

They had just pushed Gran's front door open when the lovely sound of a siren floated through the air.

The paramedics took Gran away on a stretcher with a mask over her face. Jim stayed so that Hilary could go with Gran.

"They're taking her to the mainland," said Jim.

"How?" said Daffodil. "The last ferry's gone."

"Medical helicopter," said Jim.

"Helicopter?" said Alice. "Luck-ee."

"Alice," said Jane.

"I didn't mean… Oh, never mind," wailed Alice.

Then the phoning began. Numbers written on the wall beside the phone were consulted. A muddle of long-distance and multi time zones. The parents from the east were roused from sleep. But when Kip phoned the hotel in Hawaii, there was no answer. Instead of a beep there was a person to take a message, and Kip hung up in a fluster. Jim phoned back for him and left a message.

Meanwhile, Alice found the first-aid section at the front of the phone book and began to read about heart attacks.

"We should have loosened her belt and said help is on the way. We didn't do that."

"She didn't have a belt," said Daffodil.

"We should have loosened something," said Alice, and then they both began to cry.

Jane wiped her nose on her sleeve and Alice told her to use a Kleenex and Jane said Alice wasn't the boss of her and Daffodil yelled, "Be nicer!" and Jim turned on the TV and nobody watched it.

Finally, after what seemed like hours, the hospital phoned. Jim answered. He nodded and hmmmm'ed and hung up.

"It's okay. She's stable."

Stable? What did stable mean? Kip got a flash image of Gran and horses, sleeping on hay and eating out of a manger.

"They are going to keep her overnight and do some tests tomorrow. But she must be feeling better because she sent a message to you all. She said to tell you that there is a new rule. No worrying. She said to write it on the wall."

Alice got up and pulled a marker out of her pocket. She started to print, but on the second *R* her writing got wobbly and she began crying harder than ever. Emily and Daffodil joined in.

Jim looked a bit panicked at so many tears.

"Does anybody need something to drink? I mean, cocoa or Coke or something?"

"Gran doesn't have Coke," hiccuped Jane. "Gran says Coke eats your bones up, so we would never get to be in the corps de ballet."

"Or climb Everest," said Alice.

"Or be the best of breed," said Emily.

"Cocoa, then," said Jim firmly. Then everybody revealed a talent for helpfulness and started moving furniture and clearing dishes and cleaning up the kitchen.

Jim did not insist on teeth or pajamas or proper beds, so one by one the cousins fell asleep around the living room. It was a still life of collapsed ballerinas, a sprawled dog, a bivouacking climber.

Kip sat with Jim and the sleeping girls.

"You should go to sleep," said Jim. "There's nothing else we can do tonight. Do you want to bunk down here? I can go next door and grab you a foamie."

Kip shook his head. He knew he wasn't going to sleep and he needed Operation Mitochondria. He needed a world where you could do something about the bad things.

* * *

The binder lay open on the floor beside the cot. Kip picked it up.

Enemy infiltration by Operation Mitochondria.

"What did you say just then?" Gran had asked. Then she had collapsed.

Gran knew. Of course she knew. How could he have been so stupid? Of course Dad would have shown her his story when he was a boy. It was so good. He would have been proud of it. She knew that Kip hadn't written the story at all.

He had said, "Something I wrote out," but he hadn't said it very loud. Plagiarism. Cheating. Ends and means. The end was trying to pretend that he had a talent and the means was cheating.

That discussion the first day on the beach. He knew what Gran thought about cheating. When he read the Mitochondria piece he made her so disappointed and angry that she had a heart attack.

It was his fault.

Kip threw down the binder and kicked it across the room. Kid's stuff. Stupid kid's stuff. Spies and devices and codes. Pathetic.

He turned off the light, sat down on the cot and stared into the darkness.

What if Gran died? There was no device or clever plan to prevent that.

THIRTEEN

KIP ARRIVED downstairs in the morning to a front hall full of people and a pitched battle.

"Why can't we go to visit?" Alice was wedged at the top of the hall doorway.

"I explained," said Jim. "You have to be fourteen to visit someone in intensive care. That's the rule."

"How's that fair? Is it about germs? Hilary's got just as many germs as I have. All of a sudden, fourteenth birthday and, pow, you're not germy any more?"

Mrs. Larsen appeared out of the kitchen with a plate of muffins.

Jane sat down on the stairs.

"Alice, forget it. Jim didn't make up the rules."

"Don't tell me to forget it. Since when are you the boss?" Alice jumped down from the door with a crash.

Daffodil put her hands over her ears.

"Alice, stop it. Gran might die and you're being HORRIBLE."

"So now it's my fault?" Alice thumped out the front door and slammed it.

"Muffin?" said Mrs. Larsen.

Jane and Daffodil began to cry and hiccup.

"I didn't know she might die," said Emily in a small voice.

The phone rang.

Everybody dived for it. Jim came up from the scrum with the phone wedged to his ear, waving his hands for silence.

"Yes, yes. Oh, that's good news. Yes, I'll tell them. Okay. Around noon? Yup, we'll sort it out. Thank you so much." Jim hung up the phone.

"Gran is fine. No damage at all. The doctor says it was probably an anxiety attack. She can come home this afternoon."

Jane, Emily and Daffodil jumped up and grabbed Jim, one on each hand and one on a shirt-tail. They danced around him as if he was a maypole, singing, "She's fine, she's fine, she's fine."

Kip's knees buckled and he sat down on the stairs.

Not dead. Not dead at all. Not even nearly dead. Anxiety attack. Shelve that for later.

"Have a muffin," said Mrs. Larsen. "They're blue-berry."

Jane gave a little yelp. "Alice doesn't know. I'll go find her."

The maypole gave a sniff.

"Are you crying?" said Daffodil.

"Yup," said Jim, digging into the pocket of his shorts.

"Why?" said Emily. "She's fine, she's fine, she's fine."

Jim finally came up with a tissue and gave a huge, echoing nose blow.

"Okay, you kids, I think Gran is going to need a Welcome Home card. Why don't you walk into town and buy one of those really big sheets of cardboard? They have them in the drugstore. Find the others on your way." He pulled a bill out of his wallet and handed it to Kip.

Emily bounced over to check the denomination. "Wow, we can get neon."

"Blueberry or there's also bran chocolate chip," said Mrs. Larsen.

* * *

"Can I glitter the horses?"

"Okay, except not the purple one."

Jim's money had gone a long way at the drugstore. Neon poster board, glitter glue, stickers, construction paper, craft foam, tissue paper, cellophane and food supplies to keep up the strength of the artists.

"Kip, can you do horse bodies?"

Kip shook his head. He held his marker. He couldn't think what to draw. He couldn't think what to think except—what was an anxiety attack and what would happen when Gran got home.

"Hil's the only one who can do horse bodies."

"Put the horses behind a fence."

"Pass those muffins, would you? The six simple machines are lever, pulley, inclined plane, screw, wheel and axle."

"What's that blob?"

"It's a nudibranch."

"Who ate all the red Smarties?"

Kip let the conversation wash over him in waves. He stuck a few stars to the corner of the card and started to doodle.

Jane sighed. "I don't know what to draw now."

"Draw anything that Gran likes."

"Hey, who's been picking the chocolate chips out of the muffins?"

"What are the tears for?"

"They aren't tears. They are those talk shapes. You know — in comics. When people talk. Gran likes conversation."

"What's Kip drawing?"

Kip surfaced and looked at what he had drawn. It was a ray-neutralizing gun.

"Kiiip! It's a gun."

"Gran hates guns."

Daffodil leaned right across the table to get a better look.

"You can't have a gun on a get well card, you goofhead."

Kip stared. It was the Mitochondria gun. Can convert to infarct mode, an instant source of heart attack.

Nothing he did was right. He was not a goofhead. He was a pathetic loser.

He threw his marker across the table and scraped back his chair.

"Forget it. You do it."

He caught one glance at Daffodil's shocked face before he fled.

"Kip! I'm sorry."

He slammed the kitchen door and ran up to the attic.

He stood at the door of the yurt room. The yurt looked really stupid. The binder was splayed open on the floor, its pages crumpled.

He pushed into the yurt and flipped over the cot. He slammed the legs down, pinching one finger. He gathered up his stuff and jammed it into his duffle bag. Then he ripped two twigs out of the yurt to make an opening and pushed everything into the hall.

Crawling into the yurt once more, he placed the binder in the exact middle, centered under the life preserver. He grabbed one of the supporting twigs. He pulled. It wobbled. He pulled harder and it began to crack and splinter.

He stopped. Mom had once taken him downtown to see a building demolished. A giant wrecker ball took it down in one blow, leaving rubble and a rising tower of dust.

It was awesome. Gran's house would go like that.

He locked the room and put the key in his pocket. He ran downstairs. Ignoring some cousin calling his name, he left by the front door. He looked up and down the road.

There it was, at the corner. He pulled the key out of his pocket and held it tight in his palm. He walked a short distance up the road and stopped at the storm drain. He crouched down and dropped the key between its bars.

Gone. Done. End of story.

Kip took the long way back, up behind Jim's house, through the clearing and down through Gran's back yard. He wondered if he could slip upstairs and just go back to bed.

As soon as he came around the corner of the shed, however, he heard a commotion from the front drive, cousins at full throttle. He crept down the side path and confronted a scene of Gran, almost hidden by hugging girls and a large yellow card. Behind were Jim and some other guy unfolding himself from the van.

Kip froze.

It was Orm. And there, behind him, was Mom.

What was going on?

Mom spied him and came running. "Kipper!"

She practically suffocated him in a hug. She was brown and her hair was different but she smelled the same.

"I thought you were in Hawaii."

"When we heard about Gran we decided to come back and we found a flight but we really had to scramble to get it. I've never packed so fast in my life. Look at you. You've grown."

Whoompa. Whoompa. The cousins were bending the

welcome card gently back and forth. A fine shower of glitter misted onto the driveway.

Gran's head appeared above the huddle. She looked like herself. Gran-colored, not gray. She waved at Kip.

Mom tucked Kip's head under her arm and pulled him down the driveway. Orm walked by carrying three suitcases and a pineapple. He was wearing a red flowered shirt and his face was peeling.

"Hey, Kip. Sorry about your grandmother. That must have been frightening."

Kip swallowed. The story of talent night welled up in him. He clenched his mind shut.

Stop being nice. He could spill over in a second, and the last person he wanted to spill to was Orm.

He began to pull away from Mom. "I should help with the suitcases."

Mom didn't let go. "There's enough help. I need you right here."

She felt so familiar that Kip felt he could just close his eyes and return to real life. No Orm. No making Gran sick. No enemies of freedom. Just a normal world where he knew how to be.

FOURTEEN

KIP SAT on the porch floor with his spine between two rails as everybody tried to sort themselves. It was as if the house had been given two serious shakes in the space of twenty-four hours, and now nobody knew where to settle.

At home Kip always felt he knew where to be. His family was like a portrait. There was a mother-shaped space for his mom, a son-shaped space for him and a cat-shaped space for Rocky, then Bailey, then Pinkus.

Other families were different. Jared's family, for example, was more like a screen-saver, a pattern ever changing, like when Jared's older brother's girlfriend went to Mexico in a van and she left her dog ("just for a few weeks") and then Jared's mother went away to get Auntie Fan settled in the old age home and then the school hamster came to their place for the holidays and then Jared was given a free parrot that even came with a cage and a bell. And the girlfriend never came home but Jared's mother did with five boxes of Auntie Fan's collector plates and the school hamster got lost and was miraculously found two months later and the parrot turned out to be dysfunctional and Jared's older brother got a new girl-friend and she moved right in. And the original cat and dog and brother and sister and parents moved over or spread out and figured out who slept where and who did the dishes and who got the early shower and who liked loud music and who hated toast crumbs in the peanut butter.

At Gran's house Kip had found the place to be, too — in the attic with the Operative. But now that was gone, and Gran's house didn't know what to do with him or with everybody else.

The small cousins were wound up to a frenzy, telling the story of talent night over and over, asking questions, breathing all the air, taking all the space. Every time they described Gran collapsing, Kip felt worse, until he just wanted to jump up and scream, "I did it. It's all my fault."

Mom was hovering. "Would you like a cup of tea? Cold drink? Pineapple? Orm, what did you do with the pineapple? A rest? Should I go grocery shopping?" She even tried telling the smalls that maybe they were being too rambunctious and maybe Gran was tired, but they just gave her the you're-not-the-boss-of-me stare so she gave up.

Jim leaned against the porch rail and wouldn't sit down. He kept saying that he wasn't staying but he didn't leave, either. Orm seemed to be trying to be invisible, to not occupy any space at all. This was hard because he was so big. Kip found himself half liking the way Orm's legs stretched across the porch, the way the wicker chair disappeared under him and the way he just sat still, even when the cousins did gymnastics over him.

Maybe Orm was just going to be the invisible man. Maybe it was going to be okay.

Kip caught himself. What was he thinking? He pulled himself together and concentrated on how extremely bad and embarrassing Orm looked in that extremely ugly hula shirt. What was next? Was he going to pull out a ukulele?

Hilary really was invisible, off in her room, playing her guitar.

Mom finally got someone to say yes to tea. Seconds after she went inside, Kip heard a whoop. She reappeared.

"What in heaven's name have you done to the house? Orm, go in and take a look."

Gran grinned, and the old Gran came right back. "We're releasing the inner graffiti artist. It is kind of like extreme home decorating. Don't you think it would make a great TV show? One of those reality ones? Help yourself, while you're here. The felt markers are in the sideboard."

Orm came back with raised eyebrows, a small smile and Hilary.

"Remarkable. Quite artistic. There's a wonderful map. And Hilary explained about the blues tunes."

"But…" said Mom. "What does the new owner think?"

"Doesn't care a bean. He's going to tear it down the minute we're all out of here."

"Pretty solid house to demolish," said Orm. "Don't you mind?'

Gran paused. "Two-by-fours and drywall. That's what it comes down to. And memories, of course. But those don't get bulldozed. When Herb died I decided one thing I was not going to do with the rest of my life was cling. To things and places, that is. The other thing I decided is that I didn't want to be lying on my deathbed wondering What If? What if I had lived right in the middle of a city, right in the middle of the action? So I'm going to give it a try."

Alice's head appeared upside-down from the roof of the porch. "The island is way better."

Gran smiled. "That's because you're a country mouse. But you know, I think I've always been a city mouse. I want to sit at a window and see lots of people go by. All sizes and shapes and ages and sorts and conditions. Strangers. People with secrets and surprises."

"Don't move to the city," said Emily, hopping up and down. "Just get a dog. Get lots of dogs. Dogs are full of surprises. Especially apricot-colored standard poodles."

Everybody groaned except for Orm, who made the fatal good-guest mistake of looking interested.

"Why a poodle?"

"The first reason is that standard poodles are the most intelligent…"

The conversation split, as everyone except Orm skittered away from the poodle lecture.

"If you always wanted to live in the city, how come you always lived here?" said Hilary.

"Oh, that was Pop's dream. Cut down trees. Run a boat. Have chickens. Get a truck."

"But that meant you just did what he wanted," said Hilary with a frown. "I would never do that."

"There was a time I thought that, too. But when you love somebody, you find that you want them to have what they really, really want. Herb imprisoned in the middle of the city? That would have made me too sad."

Hilary sniffed. "Compromise."

Gran shook her head. "No, compromise is when you get some kind of middle ground that nobody likes. For us that would have meant living in some dreadful suburb. Then we would both have been miserable. I'd call this more like concession."

"Ha!" said Hilary. "Giving in. That's what women do."

Gran sat up straighter in her chair. "The gracious relinquishing of power can be a great source of personal strength."

Hilary wound her legs tighter around the railings. "You're rationalizing."

Mom cleared her throat. She looked kind of panicked.

"We forgot all about the tea. I'll go put on the kettle." She fled.

Kip recognized something. He recognized himself when he first arrived.

She thinks this is a fight, he realized. She hasn't figured out that they are completely happy and can do this for hours.

The discussion rolled on and to Kip's surprise, Orm weighed in.

"Suburbs aren't so bad," he said in a deliberate way, as though talking to himself. "House of your own. Safe streets for kids. Clean."

"Prisons for housewives," exploded Hilary.

Kip left the discussion in full spate and went out to the kitchen. Mom was standing watching the kettle steam. Kip found the teapot and the tea. They slipped into their way of silence like sliding into a pair of old jeans. Mom handed him a tray and kissed the top of his head.

"You doing okay here?"

Kip nodded. "Hmm."

"Gran tells me you're building something."

Kip shook his head. "Not any more."

Back on the porch the discussion had returned to Gran moving to the city.

"And the whole point is that now I'm going to do it. I'm not going to wait until I'm too feeble and dotty to make the move. That's what you don't see, Hilary. Life is long and there is room for concession *and* assertion. There's room for country and city."

Kip handed Gran her mug, then slid back onto the floor and floated away.

What would happen now? Would Mom and Orm go back to Hawaii? Would they go home? Would they stay? Would he stay or go home? Home wasn't going to be home, either. There was going to be a new house. There was going to be a basketball hoop. He and Jared and cans of Coke and slam-dunking. No more girl cousins, no more endlessly discussing things. That was going to be excellent.

Then he thought of Alice's upside-down face, her ponytail hanging down. He still hadn't tried night swimming. They had talked about hiking around the entire island. He still hadn't met that sign-language-speaking baby.

Daffodil plunked herself in front of him and held out a cat's cradle looped between her hands.

The cat's cradle was diamonds. He pinched it and turned it into a hammock between his own hands.

"Sorry that I yelled at you this morning."

Daffodil reached into the center of the hammock and came up with train tracks. She looked up and smiled.

Diamonds, hammock, train tracks. Simple. Kip wanted to go and live in Daffodil's world.

FIFTEEN

KIP PUNCHED his pillow and turned it over. His ear-lobe was glued to his face. His toes were sweating.

It was way too hot. The back window in the attic was stuck. Whatever air there was had been long since used up and turned into carbon dioxide.

He heaved himself out of bed and looked out at the garden. There was a hint of gray dawn. A strange shape under the trees took on meaning as a plastic lounge chair. A cool, airy outdoor bed with a leafy canopy.

He rubbed his burning eyes and picked up his pillow. Abandon territory.

The house was quiet, faintly breathing in that old-house way. Kip crept down the attic stairs and across the landing.

Halfway down the kitchen stairs he heard a voice.

It was Gran.

"Have you never told him?"

Then Mom's. "I didn't see the point. Tris was fine by the time Kip was born."

Kip stopped. He sat down.

"And I didn't want him to worry. He has great memories of his father. Why complicate that? Besides, he's very young."

"I know. I know that I've been foolish to get so upset. But it just brought it all back."

"What exactly did he say?"

"It was something he had written. At first I thought it was some sort of adventure story, but then it went into this paranoid thing about people tapping the phone and getting at you through computers. And then — and this is what tipped me over — there was a bit about junk mail. It all came back to me with a wallop because that was Tristan's thing. He was convinced that there were hidden warnings in junk mail. He would collect it and highlight words and cut them out and make new messages and tell us he was keeping us all safe. We had no idea what to do. If we tried to talk to him he thought we were in on the plot. And it was so frightening for the girls. They saw their brother disappearing. We started to hide the mail. It was making us all a bit crazy."

"Yes, Tris told me."

"That was just before he was hospitalized. It was such a bad time. And then, here we were on talent night, and there was Kip, looking just like him. And being like him, too. Clever, serious, solitary, sweet. Just like Tristan before…well, before the demons."

"Oh, dear," said Mom. "No wonder you got sick. That must have been such a shock."

Kip felt as though his head was going to explode.

Dad? Crazy?

The kettle started to shriek, and he scuttled upstairs under cover of its noise.

He needed to be gone.

* * *

The backwoods path to the beach was warm and still. Ferns whipped Kip's legs as he ran along it, jumping over rocks and tree roots, grabbing tree trunks and dodging branches. When he reached the sand it tried to slow him down, sucking his feet into softness. But it couldn't. With every step he was faster and stronger.

He turned away from the sand and headed toward the rocky point. The rhythmic crunch of shell and dried seaweed quieted as he reached the rocks. Creampuff rock, bouncy log, eagle's nest. He ran fast, boulder to boulder, every step a split-second decision, every tippy sun-bleached log a quick shift of balance.

Then the cliff. The tide was up. Waves crashed against the rocky wall. Crash, sparkle and retreat.

Kip stopped. He tried to gauge the pattern of the waves. Negotiate the narrow crust of beach or climb the wall?

A large wave, bashing against the cliff and exploding white into the blue air, made his decision for him.

Climb.

He wedged his foot into a crack and grabbed a knob of rock with one hand. He pulled himself up until his other foot found a narrow ledge, then raised the first foot up to join it.

He glanced to his left. There was a promising hand-hold if he just moved sideways. It was a stretch, but he got a secure grip. A few more combinations and he was well up the wall.

It was like beach running. He was strong and capable. He was Spiderman.

Then he ran out of footholds. Firm on all four points, he looked down between his body and the rock. No, nothing for his feet. He would need to move sideways again. The only possibility he could see was a tree root. He grabbed it and gave it a strong tug. Fine.

Then, just as he was shifting his weight, the root pulled away.

A tiny avalanche of pebbles slithered down the cliff, and everything changed. Kip regained his holds, but the world came alive. The crash of the waves below him, the spray hanging in the air, the ripping scream of seagulls — he suddenly heard it and felt it. At the same time it came to him how high the cliff was when you were on it.

It was hard to breathe. He thought he could still hear pebbles falling.

He glanced up. It was too far. He needed to give up and climb back down.

The minute he released one foot and began to feel for a lower ledge, he realized how impossible that was. Climbing down, feeling the suck of gravity, was absolute-ly horrible. He would fall for sure.

One foot was trembling with tension. He forced himself to take a deep breath.

Hand, foot, foot, hand. Everything else disappeared as Kip focused on the puzzle of where next to move. Only some combination of hands and feet and rock. Hold, test and shift. Crack, knob and ledge. Only moving across and up. The magic path was there, waiting to be found.

After some minutes — or years — he heaved himself over the top of the rock face onto a grassy bed. He lay quiet for a minute, on his stomach, breathing and staring at an ant climbing a blade of grass.

Then, grabbing onto a tree, he rolled over and sat up. He watched his hands take on a life of their own. They were shaking, and he couldn't make them stop. He tucked them safely under his armpits and stared over the cliff, far away into the air.

Was it true? Had he really heard Gran say that Dad was crazy? How could it be true? The man in the photo, sitting with his ankle on the opposite knee, making a little chair for baby Kip. The carpenter who made a treasure box painted midnight blue. The lovely lad. The father who sang wake-up songs to put you to sleep. The artist who could draw a car so real you wanted to pat it like a horse.

All those puzzle pieces. The crazy piece didn't fit anywhere. The color was wrong. The shape was wrong.

Kip looked out to sea and chewed the side of his thumbnail.

Operation Mitochondria. The Suits. It was a place

where things really happened instead of just going along, where everything mattered, from junk mail to freckles. It was a good place, a good story. But to Dad it was a journal, not a story.

The teenager who cut all the labels out of his clothes because labels are a portal. He didn't just think about that, or put it in a story. He really did it.

Schizo nutbar. The words Gran wouldn't let them say.

Kip gripped the tree. The rough bark bit into his hands. He felt a big hollow open up inside him as something was ripped away. There had been a boy, and he was gone.

That Dad, the one in the stories — the one who had turned into a friend — he was just a lie. A lie told by Gran, by wrinkly Vera, a lie told and told and told by Mom. All those stories — the day Dad totaled the canoe, how Dad proposed in the reference room of the public library, Dad and the missing hamster — all those stories were lies. All the puzzle pieces were lies. They left out one thing.

This is how a crazy person totals a canoe. This is the shirt of a crazy person.

A wet nose stamped the back of Kip's hand. He jumped as a twig-festooned white dog looked up at him with the universal dog question, "Hey, hey, what's happening?"

Kip reached out and scrubbed the top of the dog's head, who woofed in gratitude. Where there was a dog, there were bound to be the dog's people.

Kip turned around. A field behind him was full of

flowers. There was a bench made of two boulders and a carved log. It was like a park.

From a distance, people sounds intruded, a booming firecracker laugh. The dog slid out from under Kip's hand and bounded up the hill.

Kip's leg began to itch and he reached to scratch it. A wet patch. Blood, trickling down his leg. He must have scraped it on the way up the cliff. He spat on his finger and wiped the blood away.

He took a deep breath and stood up, forcing his hollowed-out legs into action. Setting a fast pace up the hill, he plunged into the forest where a pink plastic tag on the tree marked a trail.

The dog people turned out to be the firecracker-laugher of a man with a toddler on his back, and two women. The dog was bouncing between the three of them. Kip strode briskly past them with a friendly hello. The toddler gave a hard x-ray stare at Kip's leg and said, "Owie." Kip felt blood trickling wetly into his shoe, but nobody else noticed and he didn't glance down. The dog followed him for a few steps until he was called back.

Kip found a really good walking stick — a sturdy one with no slivers and a knob on the top. He heard the sound of the sea behind him and the wooden croak of a raven somewhere deep in the forest. Sun through the trees highlighted a rotten log lacy with brilliant orange and yellow fungus. The path was soft with pine needles.

Kip walked with the speed and power of Marathon Man. He whacked the trees with his stick.

When he got to the road he noticed a painted sign. *Harrap's Point.*

The hike to Harrap's Point. That was one of the summer plans. Would they still do it? Could Gran? Was she really all better, or was that another lie?

Kip stabbed the ground with his stick and left it standing. That was what island people did. They left good walking sticks where other people could find them.

He trudged up the road. As long as he kept walking maybe everything could just stay still. Maybe it would always be early morning and he would always be quiet and alone on the solid dusty road. Maybe he would never have to return to the mess. The mess of the present with Orm and everything that would change at home. The mess of the past with a father who had died once and then again.

Whirr, click. Whirr, click, screech.

Kip turned and there was Hilary riding toward him on Gran's ancient bicycle. He pulled up his T-shirt and wiped his face.

"Kip, what the heck are you doing out here?"

"Nothing."

"Why didn't you say where you were going? Everyone's worried. What did you do to your leg?"

"Scraped it."

"Well, I don't have a bandaid. You'll just have to bleed. Get on the seat."

Kip obeyed.

"Don't get your feet caught in the wheels. Hold on."

Hilary stepped onto the pedals, and with one great heave they set off down the hill.

Kip held on to Hilary's shoulders. Her hair whipped back onto his face. He closed his eyes. They gained speed down the hill, faster and faster until the road leveled out and Hilary began to pedal, her shoulders rising and falling.

Worrying Gran. Kip felt his stomach knot. He had done it again. First she thinks he's a plagiarist and then...

Hey, wait a minute. Gran didn't think he was a plagiarist. That wasn't it at all. Gran didn't think he was lazy and dishonest. It wasn't his fault, Gran's collapse.

He opened his eyes and stretched his legs out wide.

It wasn't his fault.

Kip felt Hilary's shoulders tense as they made their way up the drive to Gran's house. He jumped off the bike, and Hilary dropped it onto the grass.

"Wash your leg," she called over her shoulder as she disappeared into the house. "I found him," he heard her yell.

Kip stood for a moment beside the fallen bicycle. He knew what he had to do. Gran needed to know that he wasn't crazy, and he was the only one who could tell her because he was the only one who knew about Operation Mitochondria.

He took a deep breath of summer-morning air.

Brave cliff climber. This was going to be harder than any climb.

SIXTEEN

"Everyone makes her own breakfast. The pronoun *her* includes *his*."

It was written right on the wall but nobody was paying attention as Orm stood flipping pancakes. Everyone else was crammed around the table — buttering, syruping and eating.

"Kip, where were you?"

"I went to the beach."

"You might have told us," said Gran.

"Sorry."

"What's wrong with your leg?" said Emily.

"Oh, Kipper," said Mom. "That looks nasty."

"I just scraped it on some rocks."

"First-aid box is in the bathroom," said Gran. "Wash it well."

"Can I first-aid him?" said Daffodil.

Daffodil thought three bandaids were three times as good as one, and Kip had to stop her from applying a tourniquet. When they arrived back at breakfast, Emily was in full-octane persuasion.

"There's a morning matinee of *Cats and Dogs*. Can we go? Canwe? Canwe?

"But," said Gran, "it's awfully nice weather to spend indoors."

The cousin quintet groaned.

"I don't know," said Orm, piling another pillar of pancakes on the table. "That's a movie I've always wanted to see."

Groans changed to cries of joy, and Emily looked at Orm in adoration. A plan was whipped into place.

"I believe I'll stay home," said Gran. "I wouldn't mind a quiet time with my crosswords."

"Will you be okay on your own?"asked Mom.

"I'll stay," Kip said quickly.

"Lovely," said Gran.

* * *

"Dead princess. Hmm. Diana? Nope, seven letters. Who's the Greek one? Artemis, that's it."

Kip handed Gran a mug of tea.

"Ah, you even brought lemon. Thank you."

Kip took a deep breath. There was no way into this except by jumping in at the deep end.

"I'm not going crazy."

The mug began to tremble in Gran's hand, and she set it down.

"What?"

"I know that Operation Mitochondria is just a story. I didn't make it up myself. I don't think the enemy is sending junk mail. I know what's real. It was all in the binder and I shouldn't have said that I wrote it even though I really said that I wrote it *out*, but I didn't say it very loud because I don't really have a talent, and I'm sorry that you got an anxiety attack because of that but I'm not trying to be a plagiarist and I'm not crazy."

Kip's throat closed up and wouldn't let any more words through.

Gran gulped.

"Kip. Slow down, honey. Come here."

Kip sat on the stool at Gran's feet. She leaned forward and put her elbows on her knees. She took off her glasses. Her face was close to Kip's.

"Start again. What's this about a binder?"

As Kip described his discovery of the binder and the story of the Suits and Operation Mitochondria, several kinds of weather went across Gran's face.

"...so he starts giving false information to the Suits to trap them."

"Oh, Kip, I had no idea he ever wrote this stuff down. He talked about it but I didn't know about the binder. When you read from it at talent night it all came flooding back. It was so real for him, so intense."

Gran sat back and took a gulp of tea and blew her nose. Then she looked sharply at Kip.

"Why are you telling me this now?"

"I...I heard you and Mom talking this morning, in

{142}

the kitchen." Kip clenched both fists. "She said that there was no point telling me. Why not? Shouldn't somebody know if his father was crazy?"

"Oh, Kip." Gran dug a Kleenex out of her pocket and handed it to him.

"I'm going to tell you the story of your father but first I need to say two things. It is really hard to hear when you're angry, so I'm going to number the two things and get you to repeat them. Thing one is that your mother was wrong. She and I were both wrong. We should have told you. We made a mistake. You should never have found out the way you did." Gran's voice went thin and croaky, and she cleared her throat. "Okay, what's thing one?"

It came out louder than Kip had intended, almost a yell. "You were *wrong*."

"Good. Thing two is that your father was not crazy."

"But what about — "

"I'm going to explain, but just tell me what thing two is."

"He wasn't crazy."

"Okay. Here's what happened. When Tristan was in senior high, things got very hard for him. He had been a good student, but his marks started to go down and he couldn't seem to concentrate. He seemed to lose his friends. He become very isolated."

Limited allegiances, thought Kip. He remembered the guys in the alley.

"Did he get beat up?"

{143}

Gran winced.

"Bullied, certainly. But he wouldn't tell us anything. Pop and I wondered if it was just too difficult here on the island, such a limited choice of friends. So we sent him away for a work-study thing on the mainland."

"With a photographer?"

Gran looked surprised. "Yes, how did you know?"

"It's in the story."

As Gran spoke, Kip found himself translating, peeling off a layer of espionage and eukaryotic simulators and interruption-immune remotes, peeling off a layer of story to reveal, underneath, a layer of plain, ordinary things.

"But it didn't help. He began to have delusions. Do you know what that is?"

Kip nodded. "You think things are real that aren't."

"One of the most difficult things was the paranoia, thinking that people were out to get him. The problem there was that he began to believe that Pop and I were the enemy. That's when he had to go into the hospital."

"Did they fix him?"

"Yes. It took a long time, but they finally found medication that worked for him. That's why I don't want you to think that he was crazy. He had a disease, like cancer or diabetes. And he was treated, and he recovered and he went to university and then he met your mother and he just blossomed. And then there was you and that's the story."

"Why did you think I might have that disease?"

"Oh, Kip, I just panicked. There you were, getting to

be a teenager, looking just like him and it was like he was back. And I allowed myself to get worried."

They sat in silence, side by side. Gran finished her tea.

"Kip?"

"Yeah."

"You're very brave. Coming to tell me like this. Whoopee brave, I'd say."

"It's wooka, Gran."

They both jumped when they heard the voice.

"Anybody home?"

Kip stuck his head out the window.

It was Jim, carrying a big wicker basket full of shells. He looked up.

"Present for you," he yelled.

Gran joined Kip at the window.

"Oysters! What a treat!"

"Can't stay," said Jim. "Floyd's digging his septic field today."

"Come back later then," yelled Gran, "and we'll barbecue these."

On the way downstairs to start shucking, Kip paused on the landing. Light was pouring in on Make Believeia.

Kip traced some shapes with his finger. What was that smudgy place in green? The Golden River of Stiria. An isolated mountain valley.

Kip picked up a felt pen from the can below the map. An isolated mountain valley was perfect. Hard to find and easy to defend. That would be the place.

He scanned the map for unpopulated mountain

ranges. Between Earthsea and Northanger Abbey he found it. In small, neat, prime-number printing he wrote in the space between the mountain peaks: *Project Mitochondria Base of Maneuvers.*

* * *

Dinner divided the family into two distinct camps. One camp, the wooka-sweet camp, thought that oysters were a delicious gourmet treat.

The other camp, the janky camp, found their minds edging toward one word and that word was snot. Kip thought it. Emily said it. Nobody thought to warn Orm about Emily's oyster-shucking poem and she was well launched into reciting it when Gran noticed what was happening and put her foot down.

"Enough, Emily."

"But, Gran, don't you think it takes a lot of PLUCK to eat oysters?"

"And you know that they can cost more than a BUCK to buy," said Alice, snorting into her milk.

"I love oysters," said Hilary. "I'd rather have oysters than, say, Peking DUCK."

"Unless you overcook them," said Orm, "in which case they can be as hard as a hockey PUCK."

Gran and Mom just stared at each other.

"Feel like we've lost the reins of power?" said Gran.

Later Kip decided to be helpful and take out the compost. He paused in the back yard beside the arbutus tree and thought of his conversation with Gran.

He just blossomed.

A picture flashed into his mind. He stood with his legs apart and his arms stretched as wide as wide. He tipped his head back. Big clouds were rolling across the sky, white and gray.

He held his breath. Fingers splayed, he imagined it. Leaves and flowers sprouting, bursting from the top of his head and his elbows and nose and knees and toes and every single finger. Roots pushing down into the ground, curling past the amazed worms.

A man turning into a tree or a tree becoming a man.

SEVENTEEN

THUNK.

Kip's eyes sprang open and he caught the echo of the sound. It wasn't a loud noise but it was the wrong noise for the middle of the night.

Gran's house had noises — creaking, pigeons or rain on the roof, the wind chimes on the back porch. But this was more an inside noise.

Dream or real? Kip looked down the hall from the landing to the door of the yurt room. Moonlight from the back window made its way about halfway to the cream-painted door.

Kip remembered being afraid in the night, when he was a kid. Lie as still as you can. Only move your eyes. Don't scratch that itchy little place on the inside of your left foot, that extremely itchy little place now matched by the itchy place just inside your left nostril that makes you want to rip your nose off.

Oh, get a grip. Kip gave a lurch in bed and did a double scratch. Was he Emily's age, or what?

He was just turning over and punching his pillow into a more comfortable rock when it came again.

Thunk. Then a kind of rustling.

It definitely came from the yurt room. Something was hitting the inside of that door.

Kip made his legs take him out of bed. His toes curled as they hit the cold linoleum. He raised the drawbridge. He needed an escape route if his plan…

Who was he kidding? He had no plan.

He padded softly to the yurt-room door and placed his ear against it.

"Hello?" he called softly, feeling like an idiot.

Silence. He scratched the door with his fingernails.

Thunk. He jumped away as though something was coming through. This sound was louder in volume but softer around the edges. Then more thunks and skitterings.

Kip stood frozen. He thought of the small silver key disappearing down the storm drain.

He needed someone to tell, to help.

Gran? No, Gran had been great all day but then after dinner she slumped. He couldn't wake her up.

Hilary? Impossible. He couldn't knock on Hilary's door and see her just woken up.

It would have to be Mom, and that meant Orm, of course. Could he just escape and go down and sleep on the pullout couch? No, that's where Mom and Orm were. Kip punched one hand with the other as the thunkings got louder and more hectic.

He knocked softly at the living-room door.

"Mom?" Nothing. He knocked a little harder.

Mom appeared. Her hair was sticking up above her forehead.

"Kip? What is it? What's wrong?"

"There's something trapped in the room in the attic. It's hitting the walls."

Mom rubbed her eyes.

"Can it wait until morning?"

"No. It needs to get out."

"Okay, show me."

In the attic, Mom waded though Kip's stuff and put her ear to the door. All was silent. The thing was gone or dead or hiding.

Mom waded back down the hall and sat on the cot. She turned to Kip and blinked. "Where are your pajamas?"

"I don't wear pajamas. I just wear shorts to bed."

"Oh."

There was a little catch at the end of Mom's "Oh," and suddenly Kip felt in the wrong, in some complicated, messy way.

"Sorry."

Mom gave a half-laugh.

"Oh, Kipper, it doesn't matter. Don't be sorry. It's just a mother thing. Of course, you're growing up.

Sometimes I just forget. Being away from you seemed to make that worse. When we arrived today I saw you in the doorway and I thought, Who is that immense person?"

Kip rolled his eyes.

"I guess you expected me to be standing there holding Ears-and-Claws, eh?"

Mom guffawed.

"Exactly, holding Ears-and-Claws by one ragged ear. And wearing your rompers."

Thunk.

Mom stopped laughing. "That's it?"

Kip nodded.

"Well, I guess we had better have a look." Mom made no effort to get up. "Hmmm. For some irrational middle-of-the-night reason I have two words in my mind. Those words are 'bat' and 'rat.'"

"I know what you mean," said Kip. "Like phonics. Bat, rat, cat. What about cat? Like Pinkus when he throws himself against the door, trying to get out."

"But it doesn't really sound like a cat, does it? It is too scritchy and — oh, I don't know — panicked."

"Or hat?" said Kip. "It could be one of those escaped hats, those ones that have gone wild. Escaped from the hat shelter. But you know what they say. There are no bad hats, only bad hat owners."

Mom giggled and stared at Kip thoughtfully. "It's not just that you're taller. You've changed. Those cousins have been good for you."

"Oh, pulease. Anyway, we can't get into the room. It's locked and I lost the key."

Mom stood up. "Okay. I'll call Orm."

Kip thought of the broken fridge in Hawaii.

"Right. Mr. Fix-It."

Oh, boy. The minute it was out there, hanging in the air, suspended by threads of sarcasm, Kip wished he hadn't said it. He saw the wash of hurt pass over Mom's face.

Was it rude? Had he meant to be rude? Or could they both just treat it as a joke like the feral hat?

Mom nodded.

"Yes, Mr. Fix-It. That's good. That's him."

When Mom left, Kip suddenly remembered that behind the door was not only the bat/rat/cat/hat but the yurt. His secret. The good thing he had figured out and made.

He had no time to get hold of what he felt about that when Orm and Mom arrived back upstairs. Orm was dressed in track pants and a T-shirt. No shoes. Kip wondered very briefly about the pajama issue before he shelved that whole line of investigation very far back on a high shelf.

Orm switched on the light. Why hadn't Kip and Mom thought of that? The area around the cot was revealed as a swamp of clothes, CDs and a pair of damp, sandy swim trunks.

Mom clicked into Mom-mode.

"Kip, have you done *any* laundry since you got here?"

Orm didn't appear to notice. He went straight to the door.

Thunk.

"Something's trapped, all right. No key?"

Kip shook his head.

"We can just smash it, though. Gran says we can smash things as long as they are not a bearing wall."

Orm ran his square-ended fingers over the door.

"Shame, though. Nice panel door. Not like the hollow-core rubbish you get these days."

There was a particularly loud scritching on the wall beside the door.

"Best thing is to remove the hardware, I think." Orm reached into his pocket and pulled out what looked like a very fat penknife. "We'll give this gadget a run for its money." He shook his head sadly. "Look at that, painted-over hardware. Nice brass underneath, probably. People who don't mask the hardware before they paint — what can you say."

Gran's voice appeared in Kip's brain, like a pop-up ad on the net. "Keelhauling. Keelhauling is too good for them."

Orm talked while he worked.

"We'll just dig some of this gunk out of the screw head here and see if we can get some purchase. Oh, stripped. Worse and worse. Okay, here she comes. That's one down. Now, how are we going to get at this little guy?"

Orm's tone reminded Kip of something he did himself. Talking in that smooth, even way and working away at something.

What was it?

His hands remembered first. It was brushing knots out of Pinkus. One by one, a bit at a time, no point rushing. Talking to keep Pinkus from going berserk. And so satisfying when the brush came up with a big matted clump.

Finally, with a ripping noise, Orm pulled the handle and plate away from the door. He reached inside and snicked something.

"There we go. That's my burglar act for the evening. Shall we meet our visitor?"

Orm stood aside and let Kip pull open the door. Light from the hall shone in and the yurt cast skeleton shadows. A soft night breeze blew in the partially open window.

Kip stepped in, edging around the perimeter of the yurt. Mom stepped into the doorway, and Orm looked over her shoulder.

"Kip," said Mom, "what is this?"

Where to start? A place, a room, a fort, a made secret. The world of the Operative. The world of no cousins. A territory where things fit, where all the puzzle pieces locked into place.

Suddenly, from the darkest corner there was a flutter, and a bird appeared, catapulting across the room. Kip ducked. The bird flapped and fluttered and then banged into the closed part of the window and then disappeared again into a dark corner of the room.

Mom made a small distressed noise.

"Oh, I hate this. Why can't he figure out how to get out?"

Orm sighed.

"Kip, can you open the window wider?" said Orm.

Kip shook his head. "I tried before. It's all stuck with paint higher up."

"People who paint windows shut. What can you do. Okay, here's a plan. Kip, move your arms around a bit." Orm disappeared around the corner of the doorway.

Kip did a bit of windmilling and the bird flapped out of nowhere and headed straight through the door into the light. Orm's arm shot up and caught it in midflight.

"There we go," he said. "End of bird's big night. Come and have a look."

Orm held out his big blunt-fingered hands, and a small, shiny, blue-black head poked out from between his cupped fingers.

"Starling," said Mom.

"Starling with a story," said Orm. He walked down the hall, talking softly to the bird, and knelt at the window. He reached out and opened his hands. "Off you go." The starling flapped its dark self into the dark night.

Mom shuddered.

"Why is that so creepy? A bird in the house. It is something about the noise of those little feet." She looked back down the hall. "Kip? What is that thing in there?"

Kip felt a great weariness falling around him.

"Well, there were these long sticks in the shed and then I found this drill…"

Orm's big bird-rescuing hand came down on Mom's shoulder.

"I know you two are night owls, but why don't we find out the full story tomorrow? That's enough excitement for one night for this old guy."

Mom tilted toward Orm.

"Okay. Thanks for doing that."

Orm nodded.

There was a pause. Kip knew his cue. This was the pause for a grateful stepson to thank his generous stepfather for getting out of bed in the middle of the night. But he couldn't. He couldn't make the words come out.

"By the way," said Orm, "tomorrow if you want a hand putting that hardware back on, I'd be happy to help."

It was suddenly easy.

"Okay," said Kip. "Thanks."

Kip lowered the drawbridge and lay down on the cot. He closed his eyes and imagined Orm steering Mom down the stairs.

He flopped over on his stomach and lined up three crusty socks on the floor.

Sets. With two there was only one set of two and two sets of one. But with three — Kip moved the socks around — with three there were three sets of one, three sets of two.

All summer he had been shelving the thought of

Mom and Orm as a two. The wedding. We-think. But what about the other twos?

Kip and Mom. Ketchup sandwiches, inquisition jokes, Friday night video, remembering Ears-and-Claws.

And what about the new two? Two men replacing hardware.

Maybe. Maybe it was possible.

Kip picked up all three socks. Two and three, both prime numbers.

What would the Operative make of it all?

EIGHTEEN

KIP LOOKED out the window, held his nose and tried to make his ears pop. Clouds were piled up and edged with light like a backdrop to some war of the worlds.

Ding! The seatbelt light went out and the pilot announced that passengers were free to move about the cabin.

Kip pulled his notebook out of the seat pocket in front of him. He flipped through it. He had written way more than a page a day. Mr. Fletcher was going to be totally impressed.

RAQ: Who was the first person who ever looked at a raw oyster and got the idea that it might be food?

A: A very, very hungry person.

RAQ: What personality of person is most likely to win a Monopoly tournament?

A: A smart, loud girl cousin? WRONG. My cousin Daffodil (the quiet one) beat everybody. She just bought every bit of property she could and then she showed no mercy.

RAQ: What is a good way to increase your general knowledge?

A: Get in the habit of answering a G.K. question before each meal. (Uncle Ian, father of Daffodil, the Monopoly queen, invented this system. Now Daffodil can't start eating without it.)

RAQ: Is Uncle Ian a bit weird?

A: Sufficient data unavailable.

RAQ: Why would a person who never wanted to learn to read suddenly teach herself to read, and how?

A: My cousin Emily taught herself to read using the first-aid pages in the phone book because she wanted to know "what to do in case things happen."

RAQ: What is the scary thing about night swimming?

A: Darkness underneath. Air darkness is one thing. Water darkness is something else.

A section of the notebook had some thick pages. Photos of the yurt. Orm had taken them before he and Mom went home. They looked really good. Orm had one of those wide-angle lenses. Orm said that the yurt had a very pleasing design in the great tradition of dome construction from igloos to stadiums, and that it needed to be recorded.

The back half of the notebook was blank. Kip thought of the binder in his checked suitcase, riding along underneath him. Gran had given it to him. It, too, ended in blank sheets. Just when the Operative started to suspect that Stalp and Hooveman were not what they seemed, the story ended abruptly.

The story didn't really end, though. The Operative was still playing around inside Kip's head, trying to find out the truth, trying to double-cross the double-crossers, equipping himself with really cool gadgets.

Like the alarm descrambler and the Chameleon Room. Kip looked at his hand and imagined it disappearing. That was one of his best ideas for the Operative. He turned to a clean page in the notebook and dug a pen out of his carry-on.

The Operative shone his microbeam onto the metal plate beside the door. Quickly he activated his alarm descrambler device.

The red lights on the plate scrolled up and down. Check. Then he took a sliver of explosive from its neutralizing capsule. Carefully, he inserted it into the lock. There was a soft pop. No change in the pattern of lights. Check. This was the moment. He pushed open the door and went inside.

It was the Chameleon Room. Inside was a glass stall fitted with dozens of nozzles.

The Operative stepped into the stall and turned on the switch. A fine spray covered him. Head to toe. Behind and inside his ears, between his fingers, up his nostrils and a mouthful to rinse. His clothes grew totally wet and heavy.

And then he started to disappear. Seconds later the Operative looked down at himself and he was totally invisible.

Kip shook out his hand. The only bad thing about writing was writing. He had a few things to work out, like how did the Operative get that cool micro-explosive?

But he knew where the story was going. The Operative, in his invisible state, was going to spy on Hooveman to see Hooveman make contact with the forces of evil, thereby proving that Hooveman was a double agent.

Kip decided that he was going to make the contact person look like the Lone Ethel. The Lone Ethel would make a good agent because of her lack of personal allegiances. He imagined how she would look. Her shoes would be tied on with pieces of wool. That would be a good detail.

He knew exactly where the meeting would take place. In the spring he and Mom had gone to this park near their house and there had been a huge bed of white tulips with a single crimson tulip in the middle. It stopped them both in their tracks. It would make a perfect rendezvous point for the spies.

He could see it. Crowds of tourists milling around. Kids with kites. Artists with their paintings for sale. And one quiet meeting of a forgettable man and a poor old lady — a meeting on which hung the fate of the free world.

And the invisible Operative? He would have to be careful not to touch anybody or to make anything move. The memory of the baby in the backpack at the cliff a few weeks ago jumped into Kip's mind. The noticing baby who said, "Owie." Maybe babies could see through the invisibility camouflage.

Kip looked back over his two pages. They were good. His handwriting was way messy compared to Dad's and he couldn't draw like him, but he could feel Operation Mitochondria turning into his own place, turning back into what it had been that first dusty morning—a story, a made story, a place to explore.

Kip took another stare out the window to the war of the worlds set. The movie was to come, and the meal, and he had his Game Boy and the brownies Hilary had made, but five hours was a long time. You didn't want to use up your stuff too soon.

He emptied out the seat pocket in case it contained any interesting surprises. The in-flight magazine had stories about wine and hotels. There was the safety card and the barf bag.

Barf bag.

RAQ: Where is the best place for a spy to leave a secret message on an airplane?

A: Who ever looks in the barf bag?

Picking up his pen, Kip began to write, in neat microprinting, a sequence of numbers along the top inside edge of the motion discomfort bag.

The Operative in action. Cool and clever. Saving the free world.